HIS FOR CHRISTMAS

SKYE WARREN

"Fall on your knees

Oh hear the angel voices

Oh night divine

Oh night when Christ was born

Oh night divine

Oh night divine"

—from "O Holy Night"

CHAPTER ONE

THE GUARD BEHIND the glass grunted as he pulled a manila folder from the stack. "Angel Cole," he said, sounding bored as the contents of my life slid onto the counter.

A half-empty stick of gum. A dull pencil only a few inches long.

Twenty dollars and change.

I was surprised the twenty bucks hadn't been taken by a guard, honestly. The sad collection of items didn't make me feel anything. I didn't even remember using that pencil. I didn't remember what the gum tasted like. A two year sentence had been lenient, according to the public defender, due to my age. Only two years, but it felt like my whole life—and whatever came before a distant dream.

The guard slid a clipboard to me. "Check that everything's there, and sign at the bottom."

I scanned the list and found something new had been added: a diploma. Two years had counted for something, after all. It was only an associate's degree, but it was something. With any luck, I could make a new life for myself. One that didn't involve drugs or scummy boyfriends or jail time.

I signed.

"You got a place to go?" he asked, though his gaze remained on the fuzzy TV in the waiting room behind me. The empty waiting room.

No. "I'm not sure."

He dropped an orange sheet of paper onto the small pile. *Resources for the Homeless Community.*

My chest felt tight.

I shoved everything back into the envelope but left the flyer on the counter. That seemed to catch his attention. He looked me over. His gaze traveled down and up, crawling slow, leaving chills on my skin.

"I may know someone with a place," he said slowly. "They're hiring."

My bullshit meter had been finely honed the past two years. "What kind of work?"

A humorless smile, almost a smirk. "The kind that pays."

Shame ran through me, in that deep groove where it had been so many times before. I was too broke, too stupid, too desperate to get a real job. That had been true at sixteen, and my worst fear was that it wouldn't be all that different. And now I was getting propositioned by the freaking guard. Whether he wanted me to sleep with guys or run drugs, it didn't matter. I was going to get a regular job or die trying.

Having lived on the streets before, I knew dying was a real possibility.

"No thanks," I said breezily like the dirty offer didn't hurt. "I'm heading to New York City anyway."

He snorted. "In this weather? You'll freeze."

"I have enough for a bus ticket." Totally bluffing. I had no idea how much a bus ticket cost, and I had no money for food or housing once I got there. But the odds had to be in my favor sometime, didn't it? I figured I was overdue.

"Good luck," he said, in a voice that meant the exact opposite His attention returned to the football game on TV.

Clutching the envelope in my gloveless hands, I pushed the door open. Cold blasted my face—and my body, through the thin fabric of my T-shirt. Just my luck, getting arrested in July. My clothes were no match for the December weather.

The parking lot was mostly empty, the cars parked and covered with a thin layer of snow. No one idled at the street. My daddy hadn't come. It had been a long shot, but I'd been desperate enough to write him. He hadn't answered.

Probably for the best anyway.

I really was due for that good luck, even if the guard hadn't meant it. The winter-bright sky made me squint. Chilly air skated over my skin like the guard's cold assessment of me, raising goose bumps. I shoved hands under my armpits and started walking toward a bus stop.

CHAPTER TWO

MAYBE MY LUCK had turned after all, because I found a house with a room to let in New York City. The owner of the house was an older woman with knowledge in her eyes, like she knew where I'd been and what I'd done—and didn't judge me for it. And she agreed to let me pay rent only after Christmas.

As if that weren't enough, I landed a job.

It was only a temp position, but to a girl like me it felt like a freaking miracle. *We don't usually hire people without experience*, the HR woman had said over the phone. *But one of our assistants had a family emergency and with the holidays...your application showed up at the right time.*

I smoothed my beige skirt and turned my face up to the white, wintry sky. The pale sun wrapped around the spire at the top of the building, blinding me, and I wobbled on my high heels. A cab honked at me from behind, and I jerked forward, realizing almost too late that I was standing too close to the edge.

I shivered.

"You lost?" said a thready voice.

An older man was watching me with a concerned

expression on his lined face, his dark skin a contrast to the white fluff that lined his red suit. This particular Santa manned the donation bucket right in front of the door I needed.

"Not lost," I admitted. "A little nervous."

"Ahh." He turned back to look up at the building. "You going to work for the Big Bad?"

I wasn't exactly current with the rich and famous. There were TVs in prison and the occasional magazine, but I preferred to keep my head down. But even I knew what the *Big Bad* meant. Gage Thompson was the owner of Thompson Industries. The press had dubbed him the Big Bad Billionaire after a particularly dirty takeover of a competitor.

Then there had been that unfortunate quote that had aired again and again. He'd been on an interview with some finance show as part of a "Billionaires Under Forty" feature, looking cool and crisp in a custom-tailored suit.

I don't make the rules, he'd said. *I just win the game.*

Apprehension twisted my stomach. But it was just a silly nickname, right? The newscasters said it with an ironic twist of their lips—and a wary light in their eyes.

I tried to laugh. "He's not really that bad, is he? I figured that was just, you know, for show."

The man lifted one shoulder clad in red felt. "I hear a lot of conversations coming in and out of the building. Sounds like the man lives up to his reputation."

A knot formed in my throat. "Oh."

I shouldn't be afraid of anyone after where I'd been. No matter how big or bad he was, he was unlikely to shank me while I took a shower. The worst he could do was fire me. Although if he found out I'd lied on my application, he might report me to my parole officer. The slightest offense could get me thrown back inside. I'd heard enough stories from people who'd made it out for a few months only to get arrested for some small offense. The courts weren't kind to repeat offenders.

Lying had been stupid and desperate—and necessary.

The man smiled. "Well, you won't have to see him up close, right? Young thing like you probably start at some desk far away from him."

Or not that far. From what the lady on the phone had said, I would be temping for Mr. Thompson's personal secretary. The pay would cover all the money I owed for rent, plus extra for food.

So much freaking luck I felt sick with it.

I forced a smile. "I'm sure it will be fine."

The man smiled. "That's the spirit."

I dug a dollar out of my pocket. There weren't many more where that came from, but if there was one thing I'd learned on the inside, it was that someone always had it worse than I did. Maybe by acknowledging that person and helping them, however little, I'd feel less alone.

Less lonely.

"Merry Christmas," I told the man, dropping my dollar into the slot.

"Merry Christmas to you. By the way—" he called to

me, and I turned to face him. His eyes crinkled. "Mr. Thompson puts money in the bucket every day. Always nods hello to me too. You can tell a lot about a person by how they treat people in passing."

Some of my worry cleared. Mr. Thompson couldn't be all bad. I smiled a little. "Thanks, mister."

He tipped his Santa hat. "Take care now."

✧   ✧   ✧

Have you ever been convicted of an offense or violation of the law anywhere?

I STARED AT the black letters on white paper as my heart beat a million times a minute. I'd known there'd be paperwork to fill out my first day, and with my luck, I'd known they would ask about a criminal record. Just my mumbled answer on the phone with the HR person wouldn't be enough. I'd have to put my lie down on paper, for the record.

I'd just hoped the question would be vague, maybe only asking about felony acts committed in the New York state limits while over the age of eighteen. Because then I could have truthfully answered no. My crimes had been misdemeanors in the backwoods of upstate New York, where paperwork seemed optional and rule-following even more so. And I had been a minor. Which maybe explained how they'd found no record of it when they'd run the preliminary background check the HR person had mentioned.

My hand trembled as I checked the box that said *No.*

The security guy had a sour look on his face. He spent a long time looking over my form. He even left me in the front office while he made some calls, and I squirmed in the plastic bucket seat. God, what if they found out? I'd only been released four weeks ago. Not even long enough to get used to regular food and regular clothes and regular *outside.* It seemed like he wanted to refuse me, but in the end, he handed me a freshly printed name badge and sent me to an elevator around the corner.

"Oh, thank God," a dark-haired woman said when she saw me. "I thought you weren't going to show up."

"I'm sorry," I said, too quickly. At least that much I was used to, being slow and late and wrong.

You've always been a few cards short of a deck, my daddy had said, shaking his head. *But at least you're pretty.*

The woman blew out a breath. "It's okay. Security can be a little overzealous, but that's what they're there for, right?"

"Um. Right."

Not overzealous enough, though. Because I'd passed their checks. But I wasn't going to do anything bad here. Wasn't going to steal or whatever they thought ex-convicts would do. And I definitely wasn't going to store a few boxes for my boyfriend without knowing there were drugs inside. Even if I had a boyfriend, which I didn't. Billy and I had officially broken up when his lawyer tried to argue I'd been the dealer. The judge hadn't believed that, thank God, but he'd still given me eighteen months.

The woman smiled, looking frazzled. "I'm all over the place today. I was just so worried, because today's my last day before I leave. We've only got a couple hours to get you up to speed. I'm not sure when you'll have time unless… Can you stay late?"

"Oh." I looked around, feeling a little disoriented. Everything was so shiny and reflective. It felt more like a swanky fun-house mirror ride than a place of business. I'd been so worried about getting found out that I hadn't thought much about actually working here.

"Maybe you won't have to. If you just explain to Mr. Thompson what happened, with security taking up all that time and—"

"I can stay late," I assured her. I didn't want to bother Mr. Thompson. And I definitely didn't want him asking security about me. Besides, the temp job was hourly. Staying late meant more money, and I was grateful for the chance.

"You're a doll," the secretary said, clearly relieved. "What's your name again?"

"Angel. Angel Cole."

"Angel, the thing you have to know about working here is that Mr. Thompson is harsh but fair. Some people say he's cold but…he's also generous. You know what I'm saying?"

Not really. "Sure." I tried for a smile. "Fair is good."

Especially when people had done the right thing. But if they'd lied…then the fair thing to do was to turn me in to the authorities.

My stomach turned over.

Christy gave me an apologetic look. "Just do what he says and you'll be fine. Now let me show you how the phones work."

Chapter Three

AFTER HOURS AT the desk, my neck ached and my shoulders were tense. I stretched, the cracking sound of my joints loud in the wide-open space.

Mr. Thompson had the only office on the floor, which had startled me when I first realized that. His office was spacious, as was the waiting area where I worked, and the hallway from the elevator. But still not as large as the entire building. Apparently the rest of the floor was blocked off for some other department, but you had to take the regular elevators to get there.

This elevator was reserved for the CEO. And for the two weeks that I worked here, for me too.

The Big Bad Billionaire. I hadn't met him yet, and I wasn't really looking forward to it. What if he could see right through me? With his reputation for razor-sharp intuition, he could take one look at me and know what I was hiding.

Maybe he was traveling so much he wouldn't be in the office—for two entire weeks.

Yeah, not likely. And it was also unlikely he'd be able to tell I'd been in prison just by looking at me. But sometimes I felt like my time behind bars was written on my skin, grit and grime and shame embedded into me like glass. It was always a surprise when people treated me normal, even pleasant, like the Santa outside. I stood to leave, wincing at the soreness in my legs. It hadn't even been that long, only... I glanced at the clock and frowned. Wow, it had gotten late.

And it was pitch-black through the tall windows.

I still wasn't used to keeping my own schedule. A loud bell would tell me it was time for lunch, or a guard would come round us up for shower time. But here on this floor I was alone, and so I'd kept working. As if I were some kind of windup doll that ran into a wall, unable to think for herself. *A few eggs short of a dozen,* my daddy said.

I gathered the stack of files I'd completed and carried them into Mr. Thompson's office like the secretary had told me to. But I didn't leave right away after setting them down.

Curiosity held me at the edge of his desk, let me take in every detail, every clue to the man who normally sat in that empty wide-backed chair. A plump glass paper-weight shaped like a teardrop, with bubbles inside like snowflakes. A legal pad was half torn out with scribbled writing—unreadable. And a sleek black pen, its thick cylinder shell shining as if it wasn't used much, even though I was sure it had been.

Without realizing it, I leaned across the desk and picked up the pen. It was cool to the touch, but I imagined it warm—warm from the hand that held it, stroked it. I ran my finger pad over the smooth casing. What was this made of anyway? Not plastic. Not wood. Some kind of metal?

Rich people even had different pens, and this struck me as wildly important, a sign of just how little I belonged with them, in a building like this.

My stomach clenched, and I tense, pen in hand, when I felt something brush across the back of my legs. Air. Then came the subtle scent of cologne.

I wasn't alone.

A chill raced over my skin. I would have turned, but a hand on my hip stopped me. A hand. *On my hip.* The shock of it was enough to render me frozen, and I stared down at the pen in my hand, almost accusatory, as if the beauty of it had led to this. As if this was my punishment for being where I didn't belong, for touching what wasn't mine. For lying so I could get this job.

"Thank fuck," a low male voice murmured behind me.

My mouth opened, but only a faint squeak came out. I tried again. "Excuse me?"

"They told me they weren't sending anyone." He began to stroke me, from the dip of my waist, over my hip, and trailing down my thigh. "I'm glad they lied."

The HR department? My cheeks were flaming hot...because his hand was still on my hip. His hand. My hip. My mind couldn't quite wrap itself around that. He was touching me, caressing me, and I hadn't even seen his face.

"I was getting desperate," he said, "with the holidays coming up."

I tried to imagine what desperate looked like, tried to fill in the space of his body, his face, using only his dark-whiskey voice as a guide. The picture in my mind looked nothing like the cold face that graced business magazines. That glossy image was calculated and posed. This was a warm hand on my body and breath against my hair. This was goose bumps all over my skin.

I cleared my throat. "Mr. Thompson, I—"

"No, there's no time for that. It's been too long, and Jesus, look at you. Where did they find you?"

I definitely didn't want to talk about that, about the ad I'd answered or the lies I'd told. "I needed the work," I whispered.

There was a pause where his hand froze midstroke. I held my breath, unsure whether I wanted him to stop or continue. If he stopped, he might make me leave. And the hot touch of this stranger had to be better than working the icy streets.

"I'm sure they told you about me," he said conversationally. "They were supposed to."

Who was supposed to tell me about him—his secretary? The security guard? *The man outside dressed like Santa?* And what were they supposed to tell me? That he liked to touch his secretary? Had he touched the other woman too? Or was he only touching me because I was a temp? Or maybe he'd found out about my past, found out that I'd lied, and he knew I'd have to do anything he wanted just to stay out of jail. Oh Jesus, this was too crazy. I felt crazy. With a little shimmy, I managed to step aside. I turned halfway, only to be arrested by the sight of him.

I'd have wanted him to be handsome. No, he *was* handsome, when he showed up on glossy magazines and TV news reports. He was facing the camera with a fierce expression or carefully turned away, thoughtful. Proud. Strong. Composed.

He was none of those things now.

Now he looked…hungry. Like a wolf who'd been denied too long. A wild beast staring at a doe. I shivered. "I'm sorry that I…" I glanced down at my hand, still holding his pen. I'd encroached on his territory, and now I was paying the price. "I'm sorry I touched your pen."

"Keep it," he murmured.

"Oh, I—" My gaze flickered from the pen to him and back again, and they were almost the same—both cool and dark and *belonging here.* "I couldn't."

But I couldn't let go of it either. I couldn't even move. I just stood there, holding the smooth-metal pen, feeling guilt and shame and fear. Had he thought I was going to *steal* it? He could report me for that, even if he didn't know about my record. But he didn't look angry, exactly. He looked menacing, and sure, as if he would have put his hand on my hip whether I took his pen or not. As if he knew my hip belonged to him as much as the pen did.

His eyes darkened as I met his gaze. "What's your

name?"

"Angel," I said quickly.

His forehead creased for a moment, but just as quickly, whatever question he'd had faded from his eyes, replaced by something I knew well. Lust. Desire. Possession. Men had looked at me enough times that I could recognize it.

At least you're pretty. The night I'd seen that look in my daddy's eyes was the night I'd left home, too young and too stupid to make anything of myself. At sixteen I could do little more than shack up with a guy. He'd promised me the world, but in the end all I'd gotten were two silver bracelets and a one-way ticket to jail.

Mr. Thompson was older, smarter, and a heck of a lot richer. But he might give me the same things if I wasn't careful.

"Turn around," he said, his voice gruff.

And so I obeyed him. Because I understood what he wanted from me. Because the consequences of refusing him were so much worse. And because I'd been trained to follow orders for eighteen months at the state correctional facility.

Just do what he says and you'll be fine. That was what the secretary told me. Had she meant this? Had she meant turning away and feeling him step close, shivering at the firm grasp of his hands on my hips, my back flush against his front. My eyes fell closed. Did he do this to her? Did he *think* I was her? But I had dirty-blonde hair and the secretary's was a dark brown. My breath whooshed out.

He groaned. "You're too fucking pretty, and it's been too long. I need you. Now. Do you mind?"

Did I…mind? Oh God. Was this how billionaires propositioned women for sex? By touching them, by making them burn, and then asking, almost politely, if they minded getting used? And the worst part was, I didn't know if I minded. But I knew I couldn't tell him to stop, couldn't risk him asking questions. "I'll do what you say."

He grunted in something like approval.

And I knew I *should* mind. Regular women didn't like this. A normal woman would get offended and maybe even slap him, but I'd been too well conditioned to do what I was told. Too desperate to keep this job. Both of those were reasons I let him touch me, but not the only ones.

But I didn't mind his warm hands on me or his hard body behind me, holding me up when my legs began to shake. I didn't mind seeing what else he could make me feel. The truth was, I was starving for human touch. After two years behind bars, I hungered for it. Feared it. Needed it. But when his hands slipped back to cup my ass, I tensed.

The pen fell, almost silent, on the plush carpet.

"Am I going too fast?" he murmured. "Christ, of course I am. I'll make sure you're ready for me. It won't hurt."

It seemed like such a small thing to offer me. *It won't*

hurt. And such a huge gift. I felt offended and grateful at the same time, shamed and eager, and my body reacted by pushing my ass into his touch. He squeezed, and a moan escaped me, low and needy, as he pulled me against his body, showing me his arousal in the hard brand of his erection.

He hissed at the contact. "Jesus." His hands moved from my waist, skimming over my shirt. "I want to make you feel good. Can I do that? Can I make you come?"

He was asking...*permission?*

Something about this seemed off—that he'd touch me like he had every right to but ask almost meekly if he was allowed to make me come. The world felt off balance, but I didn't question it. I couldn't question it, not with my employment and my housing and my freedom at stake. Couldn't question the sudden relief that ran through me. The thin cots and cool metal chairs in prison hadn't felt good. The bare walls and coarse sheets on my bed didn't feel good either. But he could make that pain go away. He would make me feel good, I knew he could.

Two minutes in his arms and I already knew so much about his skills in this department. This was a form of interview, his hands cupping my breasts, broad fingers finding my nipples through the fabric.

"Please," I whimpered.

He stroked my breasts with agonizing gentleness, weighing them in his hands, lifting them, and squeezing softly. Warmth coursed through me, heating me inside the confines of my clothes. My arms were trapped beneath his, and it was a relief. A relief to know I didn't have to move—that I *couldn't* move. He was directing me, commanding me. This was a man used to being obeyed, and power coursed through every caress of my breasts.

His breath whispered across my temple. "More?"

It wasn't enough. Not after two years of impersonal touches from the guards or dirty looks from the other inmates. Not after coarse uniforms and cool concrete and smooth metal bars. "Mr. Thompson, *please.*"

His cock seemed to surge at my words, flexing against my ass, as if it were punching through so many layers of fabric, as if it could push inside me. My inner muscles answered by squeezing around nothing, and I knew my panties would be damp. And still he only touched me, caressed me, stroked me outside my clothes. It felt too dirty and not dirty enough. I was breathing hard, each intake of air pushing my breasts into his hands. The friction made my nipples peak, ready for him to grab.

And he did grab them, so carefully, between his forefingers and thumbs. The thin fabric of my bra and my shirt barely hindered him at all when he pinched me, and I cried out, pressing my legs together.

"Pretty," he murmured, and the word made me shudder, close enough to what my daddy had told me. "These are so pretty. What color are your nipples, sweetheart? They're going to be wet from my mouth before this night is over. You know that, don't you?"

"No," I said, almost a moan. I had no idea what he would do to me or how far he would go.

His hands paused. "Can I see you, Angel?" he asked, his voice raw. Almost pleading. "Let me see you."

In answer, I let my head fall back on his chest and closed my eyes. *Let him.* I could let him do anything. I wasn't sure I could do much more than that, but I could lean against him, using his strength, while his hands undid the buttons of my shirt. He pulled the sides apart, and cool office air rushed over my skin, raising goose bumps.

He sucked in a breath. "Fucking pretty."

He must have been telling the truth when he said it had been a long time. A man like him would be used to gorgeous women who had the best diets and makeup and clothes. My bra was from the dollar bin, made of cheap beige satin stretched in the wrong places. I shouldn't have been anything special to a man like him, but he sucked in a breath and stood unmoving. He must have been staring at me. Must have been…awestruck.

Or at least luck-struck, and for me, that was close enough.

When he reached one hand into my bra cup, my body slid closer to him, his hold on me almost too tight—and perfect, like that. I reveled in the feeling of being pressed against him, within the embrace of his body, the unbreakable hold of it. He was all hardness and strength, all confidence and a deep, endless well that only my body could fill.

Without my consent, my hips rocked against his, and he responded almost violently, pushing me forward, his cock an almost painful rod against my hip, his fingers tightening around my breast.

He made a rough sound as he exposed me fully, tugging down the cups until my small breasts plumped. I looked indecent like that, breasts thrust forward, begging for his touch—but then I was indecent. I was filthy and shameful and somehow aroused. My blood rushed so fast all I could hear was the beat of my heart, and his.

Instead of cupping my breasts again, he tugged my skirt up.

"Just a little more," he muttered, and I wasn't sure if he was talking to me or himself.

Then it didn't matter, because his fingers slipped inside my panties. The shock of his rough skin in my private place made me gasp. I pushed up on my toes, but the high heels didn't leave me anywhere to go. I was caught by his arms and my shoes, pinned in place as his fingers stroked through my folds, finding dampness, finding need.

"It's been...a long time," I gasped, because I needed him to know that. Needed him to go slow. Needed him to go *fast,* because oh God, I was dangling over the cliff, already there.

He groaned. "Then how...?" He pressed his mouth down my neck. "Never mind. Don't answer that. You don't have to say that stuff. You don't have to lie."

"What?" But then his fingers found my clit, and I shuddered, helpless, unable to demand answers, unable to do anything but rock against his hand in an age-old rhythm. I was like the ocean, pressing against the beach with every wave, feeling rough sand sift through my slickness.

And I couldn't have stopped him for anything. Not the sun, not the moon. Not even for the temp job I needed so badly.

"I want to make you feel good, that's all," he murmured against my neck. He nipped at my earlobe, and I jolted in his arms. Then he reached lower, dipping his fingers inside, this thumb stroking my clit. "Want to make you feel good," he repeated, again and again, while the waves crashed and I finally broke, coming apart around his callused fingers, crying out his name. *Mr. Thompson.*

Then there was only the ragged sound of my breathing. Soft caresses brought me down slowly, like he knew how tender I felt, how vulnerable.

How afraid.

He pulled his hand from my panties, and before I could register what he was doing, he pressed his fingers against my lips. "Taste yourself," he ordered gruffly.

I opened my mouth—to protest?—but he pushed inside, swiping the musky flavor on my tongue. I closed my lips around him and sucked his fingers clean. I'd never done that before, but it felt right. It felt especially right when he made a choked sound that I knew was arousal. I slicked my tongue against the seam of his fingers and closer to the tips, pretending they were his cock, miming the actions I'd use to pleasure him and lap the precum from the head.

But he didn't spin me around then. Didn't push me to my knees like I thought he would. Wasn't that what rich men in suits wanted from the women around them?

Instead he gently straightened my bra so it covered my breasts and began buttoning my shirt. I was still half-delirious from the orgasm. I was completely dressed by the time I could speak.

"What about you?" I whispered.

He stepped back. I couldn't see him move, but I could hear him, *feel* him, as he removed his strength and warmth. And then I was standing alone. Again. Reeling from an orgasm I should never have had.

"I'm fine," he said in a clipped voice that proved his words a lie. He was *not* okay, and it was my fault. All of this was my fault, because I'd sneaked into this situation, clearly unprepared.

I whirled to face him. "What *was* that?"

It shouldn't have been that hard to figure out. The big bad billionaire had taken what he wanted from the secretary. If I kept working here, he'd probably keep taking it from me, again and again. Why did the thought of that make me clench? I should be horrified, disgusted. I should be angry, but when I looked into the dark, troubled eyes of the man in front of me, all I felt was anticipation.

"I mean we're finished," he said gruffly. "You've done your job. Now get out."

My eyes widened as hurt lanced through me. I should be running out the door. Heading straight to the HR department to tell them I quit. But all I could think was, *You promised my nipples would be wet from your mouth.* He hadn't tasted them yet. I hadn't tasted him yet either. How could we be done?

He didn't want to be done.

I could see that in the stress around his mouth. Tense, because he hadn't gotten any relief tonight. Not yet.

I stepped closer, and I could almost feel his wariness. "What are you doing?" he asked, his voice clipped.

"I'm returning the favor."

"That's not how this works." He swore softly. "They're supposed to give you instructions."

Well, they hadn't. Did that mean he touched all his secretaries? The thought made me tense, even though it shouldn't have been a surprise. "What instructions?"

His eyes hardened. "That you do what I want. And don't ask questions."

My hands clenched into fists at my side. I hated being helpless… although I felt most comfortable that way, with a guard telling me where to sleep and what to eat and when to bend over. And I liked it too with a stranger telling me when to come. He'd proven that much, and I hated that my own body seemed to have turned against me. Tears pricked behind my eyes.

He leaned forward, placing two fingers under my chin—the two fingers that had just touched me intimately—and looked me in the eye. "It's not personal, Angel. I request a girl when I need one. I use her until I'm done. Understand?"

I swallowed hard, not breaking eye contact. It was just business, the way he'd cupped my breasts and slid his fingers deep inside me. Just business the way he'd groaned into my hair. But no one could be that cold, even him. Especially him. I stared into those murky depths, wondering what pain he was hiding. "Yes, sir."

His eyes flashed white-hot, and I knew he liked me calling him *sir*. But when he spoke, his words lacked any of the warmth he'd imbued into every touch. His hand dropped away, and I lost even that bit of connection.

"Now tell me, Angel. What happens next?"

Leave. He wanted me to leave. He also needed me to stay. I felt that in every cell of my body. But it wasn't my job to fix a lonely billionaire. I didn't even have that power if I wanted to.

"And tomorrow?" Because I really did need this job, and I hated the idea that I should have to suffer—and possibly get evicted—just because he had intimacy issues.

"What about tomorrow?"

"Do I show up to work?" Anger rose up in me, even if I didn't have the right to feel it. "And you could maybe tell your HR department not to bother with the background checks and all that if you only want people working here for one day."

His eyes flashed, and I remembered exactly why I'd thought he looked mean. He looked more than mean; he looked terrifying. My heart pounded in my chest, so heavy it felt like it must be visible through my clothes—but he wasn't looking at my chest anymore. He looked directly into my eyes.

"What did you say?" His voice was deceptively soft.

"I said…" My accusations faltered. He may have done something callous, but I had no right to call him on it. I should walk away with my head held high and count this as a lesson learned. And I would do those things, but I felt myself breaking down under the stress of the past few months. And years. Living on the streets, getting caught, prison. And then after, wondering if I'd made it this far for nothing, if I'd starve before the New Year even came. That orgasm had unwound something in me, something vital, something that made me lash out. "The HR person said this was a two-week job. I don't have anything else lined up."

"The HR person," he said, his voice sounding strangled.

"This was the only job I've found in weeks. I know it's not your problem, but rent is due. And my fridge is empty. I *need* this job." Bitterness shadowed my voice. "And it turns out you only wanted me for one night. For *this*."

He walked stiffly to the window and looked out. His silhouette was tall and imposing, even against the impressive backdrop of the city.

"I worked hard today." I didn't know why I was explaining myself to him. It seemed important that he understand. I was *willing* to work hard. "I can do this job while your secretary is out. I won't screw it up if you let me stay."

"Christ," he said.

My chest tightened with humiliation. And fear for what I'd do next. Was this what I'd been reduced to? Someone to get called in, to fuck and then discard? Was this my life now? My throat felt thick, and I had to force the words out. "I'll just go now."

Leave, like he'd told me to.

"Wait, Angel. Is that your real name?"

I turned back, my hand on the door. "Yes, Angel Cole."

He looked pained. "Ms. Cole. I've made a mistake. A big mistake." The words sounded so rusty I knew he hadn't used them often. He probably hadn't made a mistake in years.

And I still didn't know what he was talking about. "Sir?"

He turned and gave me a half smile. Or a snarl. "You weren't supposed to go through HR. You were supposed to be sent by the discreet agency. A very expensive, very exclusive agency with a stable of girls who are trained to do what I tell them to. But you weren't, were you?"

I shook my head silently.

A rough exhalation of air. "You weren't sent for me to use. Not like that."

From the guilt on his face, I knew he meant what he'd said. He had thought I was some kind of escort sent for him. And he really didn't know about my criminal record. My secret was still safe. "It's…it's okay."

He grimaced. "It's not okay. I forgot my secretary was going on vacation. It wasn't planned, so I didn't… I just saw you standing in my office and assumed…"

Because I looked like an escort, apparently. Heat flooded my cheeks. "So can I keep working here?"

He faced the dark windows, and all I could see was his reflection, almost haunted. "It's late," he said finally. "Go home."

"And tomorrow?"

He glanced back. His gaze met mine, eyes as flat and cool as the glass behind him. "Tomorrow I'll figure this out."

CHAPTER FOUR

I BARELY SLEPT that night, very aware that he could figure *me* out come tomorrow. Figure out who I was, figure out that I'd lied. And then the fact that there'd been a misunderstanding in his office would only be foreplay for my return journey to prison. Wham, bam, and thank you, ma'am. Lying on an application may not be a crime... but lying about my criminal record was a crime.

There was something else that kept me tossing and turning: complete and utter humiliation at my reactions to him—all while he'd thought I was a prostitute. The temp job was only for two weeks, but I'd managed to make a mess of it in a single day.

Or maybe he was as embarrassed as me. Maybe he'd pretend the entire thing never happened.

By four a.m. I gave up on sleeping and got dressed. At least I could actually finish that stack of files Christy had left for me before Mr. Thompson figured me out and fired me. At least my security badge still worked. The floor was still dark when the elevator opened at five a.m. Floor-to-ceiling windows revealed the city skyline still dark with night. The walls were smooth—no light switches—but the glow from my computer monitor gave me enough light to work.

I worked through a few of the files before a sound distracted me. Had that come from Mr. Thompson's office? I went back to work, trying to focus, hoping it would be enough to keep this job...

That noise again.

I walked closer. The door was open, and the overhead lights were off just like the rest of the floor. It looked empty. So what had made that sound? Or who?

It didn't escape my notice that this was exactly how I'd gotten in trouble last time—going into the boss's office while he wasn't here. But I had to see for myself, make sure everything was okay, now that I'd heard a sound.

It was a little spooky on the floor all alone.

But it turned out the boss *was* here. He was sitting in his chair, wearing what appeared to be the same suit as last night, or maybe he had an entire closetful of custom-tailored suits. This one looked a little more rumpled than last night, tie loose, the top button undone.

His head rested on the leather back of his chair, and his eyes were closed. Was he sleeping?

I started to back away without making a sound.

"Come in, Ms. Cole."

Okay, not sleeping. I took a deep breath. "Good morning."

"Sit down."

I sat. *Oh God.* He was going to fire me. That was the

only explanation for him wanting to talk to me about it. So much for pretending it never happened.

He opened his eyes—and even in the shadows I could see he looked furious. And terrifying, all over again. Whatever softness I'd imagined while he'd touched me was gone now. In its place was only Gage Thompson. I'd faced down people who wanted to hurt me with my chin held high. I had to, because weakness only made them hurt you longer. But they were junkyard dogs to his big bad wolf. Deep inside I began to shake.

"Mr. Thompson, about last night—"

He stood and circled the desk, and I couldn't help it—I cringed back. His expression was too angry. He looked exactly like the Big Bad Billionaire. I didn't think he'd hurt me, but I hated the thought of him being angry at me. I had always been a people pleaser. It was just how I was built. I would have done anything he said.

He set something down in front of me on his desk. His phone, black and sleek and forbidding.

"You can call from here."

My voice trembled. "Call who? The temp agency?"

"I suppose you should call them too, after. But no. I meant the police."

Fear spiked inside me. No no no. He must have realized who I was. Had he already reported me? Or was he waiting for me to call, to turn myself in? I couldn't do it. "Please no," I breathed.

"The police," he said, his voice clipped. "I'll leave the room if it makes you more comfortable. I'll remain on this floor, so they know where to find me."

"To find… you?"

"You can wait here, of course. You'll be comfortable. I won't bother you."

Uncertainty wove its way around my limbs and chest, a tight sort of comfort. He was telling me to call the police and assuming they'd come here. But why was he being so solicitous while he did it? Why would it matter that the criminal who'd lied to him was comfortable?

"Mr. Thompson," I said slowly, "I know I'm not the brightest bulb. But it almost sounds like… like you want me to call the cops on you."

"That's exactly right, Ms. Cole."

"Angel," I corrected absently. "But *why* would I call the cops on you?"

"Because I raped you."

He did *what* to me? Shock held me breathless for a moment. I couldn't even feel relieved that I was off the hook, because this was too crazy. I blew out a breath. "No, you didn't."

"I did."

"I was there. I would have noticed."

He cleared his throat. "I penetrated you with my fingers. Without your consent. You need to report me. I won't contest it."

Penetrated with his fingers. God, it sounded so cold. And somehow hot. But regardless of how he said it, he hadn't hurt me. "It wasn't against my consent."

He made a scoffing sound. "Of course it was. You wouldn't have let me touch you. A stranger. A stranger like me." Before I could even ask what he meant by *like me,* he continued, "But you knew I was the boss. You felt coerced. Of course you did. Anyone would."

"Well, I'm glad you have me all figured out, but it's not true." Not to mention that even if it had been against my consent, I would hardly be calling the cops on him. That would only expose the fact that I'd lied to get this job.

"You didn't feel coerced?" An eyebrow rose. "You didn't know I was the boss?"

Heat rushed to my face. Of course I'd known he was the boss. He only had to speak, only had to stand behind me, only had to put his hand on my hip, and I'd known who was in charge. "I let you touch me because... because I was surprised, at first. And then I was confused. And then I didn't want you to stop."

His brow furrowed. "Why not?"

Because I didn't have a choice. But that would only prove his point. And besides, it wasn't strictly true. "It felt good," I whispered.

For a second his eyes darkened, and I knew he was remembering the feel of my body climaxing against his fingers, the sounds I made as I came. He shook his head as if to clear it. "Whether you enjoyed it or not isn't the question. What I did was immoral. If you won't call the police, at least call the workforce commission. Or human resources."

He wanted me to report him to his own employees? I blinked. "I'm not going to tell anyone what happened."

He ran a hand through his dark hair, clearly frustrated. "Jesus. I never wanted this to happen."

Never wanted to accidentally finger his secretary? It seemed like a very specific worry. "I don't understand."

A humorless half smile twisted his lips. "It's irony, that's all. The thing I was doing to prevent the problem led to the problem."

"You're not making sense. And I'm not very sharp to begin with, so could you please just… explain it to me?"

He frowned. "You keep saying that—that you aren't smart. Why?"

My stomach tightened. "Don't change the subject. Why would you think you hurt me? Why would you think you *would* hurt me?"

He studied me for a moment, then blew out a breath. "I'm not surprised that I'd hurt you. I hate myself for it, but I'm not surprised."

My blood ran cold. "What do you mean? Have you hurt a woman before?"

I knew for damn sure he hadn't raped me last night—whether he believed me or not. But he still could have hurt some other woman. Maybe that was why he was so afraid to do it… again.

His jaw tightened. "No, but I could have. Every so often I need…" A sound almost like a growl escaped him. "I need to use and to hurt. I need… fuck, I need relief. And I *won't* risk it with a woman I know and care about. I use a service, and every woman that signs up knows exactly what she's getting into."

A small sound escaped me. Of surprise. Of disgust? But not at him. At whatever strange darkness he felt he had to hide. That he put himself through this just to take care of ordinary needs. Needs like sex. Like human touch. Like intimacy.

"They tell the women what to expect, make sure they understand the kind of man they're coming to service. I pay them above their asking rate to compensate for the risk." He paused. Regret flashed through his eyes. "Not like you."

"Mr. Thompson. It doesn't have to be that way."

"It does," he snarled. "Last night proved that. It proved I'm an animal who can't even ask what you're doing here. Can't even figure out whether you're there to file papers or fuck me. I just saw you bent over, and I *wanted* you, and I took you."

I knew from his voice how much that hurt him, the thought that he'd acted on impulse. He held himself so rigidly, left no room for error, pretended he wasn't even *human.*

"So tell me what you want," he said, his voice rough. "If you won't report me, let me repay you. Money, a car, anything. Name it, and it's yours."

I couldn't help but gasp. "I don't want anything."

"There has to be something." His voice sounded tight, like a steel cable in a bridge, holding thousands of pounds of metal and cars, keeping the two sides of land apart. What would it take for him to snap?

I closed my eyes against the need in his expression—need to atone for ever touching me? Or need to touch me again? "Can we pretend this never happened? That's what I'm asking for, Mr. Thompson. Let me finish my temp position. That's all I want."

And if my voice trembled on the lie, he was kind enough not to mention it. "Then stay," he said instead, gruff and almost angry. "Stay."

CHAPTER FIVE

I KEPT MY head down for the next week, working through the files Christy had left. I also answered the phones and greeted visitors who met with Mr. Thompson. Despite that, I didn't have much interaction with him. By tacit agreement, we spoke quietly to each other and with the minimum amount of words. Even when I'd hear him yell at some poor asshole who'd overpromised or underdelivered, he would always speak to me courteously and succinctly.

Thank you, Ms. Cole. If you please, Ms. Cole. It was like he'd never had his hands under my bra or inside my panties. As if he'd never spilled what was obviously his darkest secret to me.

We were strangers, as we *should* be, but it still felt like a loss.

The only other room on this floor space besides his office was the supply closet. Closet wasn't really the right word—it was bigger than the bedroom I had rented. The whole building was spacious, but this area, the secured area reserved for the CEO, was an oasis of space, so much space I sometimes felt choked up with it, as if my body didn't know how to react to open air without bars or grime or violence to block me in.

I spent a lot of time in the supply room struggling with the copy machine. It spit out page after page of nonsense characters in rapid fire, the case hot to the touch. I pressed the buttons to make it stop, almost frantic, but it wasn't listening to me. I wasn't great with technology. I was good with people—but the only person here was avoiding me.

Sighing, I pulled the stack of printed pages out. The question marks and strange diamond boxes mocked me. Totally ruined.

I tossed them into the recycle bin.

The copy machine blinked red. Out of paper. Of course it was. And I needed to try over again with this print job, so I went to the metal shelves to get a new ream of paper. Up high, almost out of reach, but I barely got ahold of it and dragged the box closer, tipping it over the edge, almost there, balancing the heavy weight of it on my fingertips...

A throat cleared behind me.

My heart jumped, and the box slid from the shelf, off balance, falling down onto me. I flinched, expecting to be hit. Arms reached around me and lifted the box. A wisp of air was all I felt. I whirled to face a grim Mr. Thompson.

His face was set in stern lines, mouth a brutal slash. His eyes glinted like a threat. "You could have hurt yourself," he said. "You should have called me."

Call the CEO of a major corporation to help me get

a box down? Not likely. "I had it."

He set the box on the floor as if it weighed almost nothing. His eyes took in everything—my disheveled appearance, blouse tight around my breasts, skirt a little higher than usual because I'd been reaching up. They took in the pile of ruined pages in the recycle bin too, and I rushed to explain.

"I sent the file, and it worked once. Then when I hit the Repeat button it just started—"

"The thing's a menace," he said almost absently, dismissing the problem. Instead he focused on *me,* like I was the problem. Like I was a menace. I took a step back, but there was nowhere to go. The coolness of the metal shelves seeped through my clothes, sending a shiver down my spine.

"I'll fix it," I said, too quiet.

His eyes were dark, expression severe. "Don't."

"Don't what?"

"Don't look at me like that. I'm not going to hurt you."

"I know." But I looked away, and I knew he didn't believe me. I wasn't afraid of him hurting me. I was just plain afraid. I'd lived my life like that—afraid—and I didn't know any other way to be.

"Angel." He looked surprised at himself, rearing back, snapping himself back to the formality where he was clearly more comfortable. "Ms. Cole."

He seemed massively uncomfortable, holding himself stiffly, not quite making eye contact anymore, and it made me want to go to him. To reach out to him. But the years had taught me not to. They'd taught me to be wary. "Mr. Thompson?"

"I want you to know… what happened that night. I don't do that often."

I wasn't sure what he meant. He didn't feel up his secretaries? Or he didn't hire a woman to visit him in his office, late at night, when everyone else was home. "Okay."

"I only do it when I can't—when I need—It's not that often."

I wondered if he knew how much he'd revealed, that it was a struggle for him. That he put his needs last.

"Why does it matter what I think?" I asked softly.

His voice was gruff. "I don't know. But it does." He turned away to look at the copy machine. And those awful ruined pages, proof of just how incompetent I was, how little I deserved even this temp job. "Maybe because I disrespected you, and I'd like your forgiveness."

"There's nothing to forgive." My throat tightened. I had no right to his past, his privacy, when I kept my own secrets. But I wanted to know. "I just… Why do you think you need to do that? To hire someone?"

I didn't bother mentioning that he was handsome or rich. Or that he could do amazing things with his hands. He was too self-aware not to know those things. But he'd picked an almost painfully impersonal way to fulfill his needs instead, and curiosity had eaten at me all week.

There was a long pause, and I almost thought he

wouldn't answer. "I don't talk about this much." A self-deprecating smile. "Don't talk about it ever, really. I suppose if anyone deserves the full story, it's you. And maybe then you'll be convinced you need to report me."

He crossed the room and leaned against the shelf, giving me a clear path to the door. All his grace fled, and he seemed so weary, as if the walls and floor and metal rebar in the building were holding him up—instead of the other way around.

I raised my chin. "I won't change my mind."

"My father was Benedict James." He seemed to be waiting for a sign of recognition.

I shrugged helplessly. The name meant nothing to me.

"He was a serial murderer." He looked down. When he met my gaze, his dark eyes were filled with pain. "And a serial rapist. He raped and murdered seven women that they know about. Because they found the bodies."

Shock stole the air from the room. "That's horrible."

His expression was stark. And etched into him.

"There was one other woman, except she survived. She managed to escape his cabin and get to the road. She got herself free."

My stomach dropped. I knew where this was going. He'd already told me how the story ended—with him sitting in front of me, hating himself. "I'm so sorry," I whispered.

I wasn't sure he could hear me. "Not completely free, though. Turned out she was pregnant. She decided to keep the child. I'm not sure why. Back then abortion wasn't as accepted or available. And adoption…well, for whatever reason, she kept me."

"She loved you," I whispered.

His gaze met hers. "Did she? I suppose so. She tried to raise me right. To understand the difference between right and wrong."

"You do understand, Mr. Thompson. The fact that you're worried about me proves that much."

His eyes seemed to burn. "She gave me her last name and left the line on the birth certificate blank, so the press never found out. And I've tried to keep myself away. To keep myself locked up. In this office, in my penthouse. Away from people I could hurt."

Oh God. "You didn't hurt me."

He'd touched me. He'd made me come. But he hadn't hurt me. He also hadn't done anything for himself, stopping before he could get off, stopping before he knew he'd made a mistake with me.

He cleared his throat. "I use the service when I need it. To keep myself in check."

I laid a hand on his arm then. I couldn't stop myself, even knowing I might get burned. Almost wanting it. "You don't have to do that. You're a regular man, capable of… doing regular things."

Regular sex. Regular relationships. And I almost laughed at myself for the sad spark of hope deep inside, as if he might have regular sex with *me*. A regular relationship. With me.

He shook his head, gaze locked on mine. "Maybe this is all I have time for."

If that were true, if he really preferred this, then he wouldn't feel the need to justify it. And he certainly wouldn't make the appointments so spread out that he was dying to be with a woman, so hungry for one that he didn't even notice she was wearing the most old, threadbare clothing. Like I had been.

"I don't think so." I had no right to tell him anything, but the tortured look in his eyes wouldn't let me stay quiet. I raised my chin, stubborn. I could be stubborn when it mattered. He mattered. "I think you want more. And you deserve more."

A curious light passed through his eyes. No, curious was too benign a word. This look was determined. This was the way he might look at an opponent across the boardroom, digging deeper and deeper until he'd found their weakest spot. "Why are you so understanding of this? I think most women would have reported me. Or at least quit."

"I don't know if that's true. I'm not that special." Ignoring his doubtful look, I continued. "But I know what it's like to have people make you feel bad for things that are true—and things that aren't."

He looked almost amused. "No one's trying to make me feel bad, Angel."

He didn't seem to notice the slip of my real name. "You're trying to make yourself feel bad, Mr. Thompson. But the thing is, I'm not going to let you."

He opened his mouth. Closed it. "Nothing special. Is that right?"

My cheeks heated. "That's right," I said, pretending like I had no idea what he was talking about. It wasn't hard to pretend. Often enough I didn't know what people were talking about.

"I think I'm not the only one trying to make myself feel bad," he murmured.

I thought in that moment that he saw me better than anyone ever had. That he *wanted* to see me more than anyone ever had. His head bent toward me... *He's going to kiss me.*

He didn't kiss me.

He licked my lips instead. I parted them on a gasp, and he bit my bottom lip, tugging it and worrying it between his teeth. Then he slipped his tongue into my mouth, sliding it against mine.

It *was* a kiss, the most carnal kiss I'd ever gotten. Like animals mating. And I realized that the nickname *Big Bad Billionaire* must have been given by someone who had met him, maybe even by someone who had been fucked by him, because it completely applied to this. He was a wolf. He'd hunted me, he'd taken me down. And now he devoured me.

I let him. I did more than that—I kissed him back. I wrapped my arms around his neck and pulled him down to me, to my level. His hands went under my skirt, curving around my ass and lifting one thigh so that when he pressed me against the copy machine, my sex was flush against him. Even through the clothes I could feel his erection. Feel the heat of him.

That wasn't enough for him. Not enough for a man used to taking what he wanted.

He lifted me onto the copy machine, so I was sitting on it—no, lying down on it. He spread me out and stole my panties. He took over my body with the control and precision he must apply to business, and I was bared to him, spread open, left without any defenses.

He stared down at my pussy so long I began to squirm, acutely aware of the hard plastic lid I was lying on top of. My head barely rested on the edge of the copier. When his eyes met mine, they were molten—dark, almost red, or maybe that was just the reflection from the Empty Tray light.

"I can't wait to taste you," he said, his voice low, and excitement raced through me. Especially when he leaned down and placed his mouth against my lower lips—oh God, especially then. He kissed me there without any hesitation or delay, as if he really couldn't wait, as if he needed to lap at my tender skin, as if he was desperate to press his tongue between them and draw out my juices.

His moan vibrated through my skin, the movement almost excruciating against my clit, in the very best way. My legs stiffened in reaction, falling off the edge of the copier. He caught them and put them on his shoulders. His hold on my thighs widened me, opened me to him, so he could press his face even deeper against me, sliding his tongue up and down the slick folds until I thought I would scream.

"Please, please, please," I moaned.

His gaze met mine. "What do you need, Angel? Tell me."

He wanted me to say it, and just the thought of it, the faint humiliation of begging and the prospect of being denied, made me clench. He noticed—because his finger was inside me now. He'd slipped it in when I was busy writhing against his mouth, so wrapped up in his tongue and my clit that I'd hardly noticed the intrusion. But I noticed it now as my muscles squeezed him tight, just that one finger—how would it feel to have something thicker? Like two fingers, three? Like his cock, pulsing and heavy, wrapped with latex and shoved inside me?

"Make me come," I whispered.

His expression was strained, almost desperate, and he went at his task like a man starving. He ate at my pussy with harsh, angry strokes, using his lips and his tongue and even his teeth to bring me to the edge.

"Not yet."

I gasped a breath. "Mr. Thompson."

He groaned. "Jesus. Not yet."

It took all my strength not to come, all my willpower as my body surged toward orgasm, hovering on the brink. I shuddered on top of the copy machine, writhed against the plastic made warm by my body, almost turned on by the faint texture of the casing, by the cool wash of air from the vent above us. Every touch on my skin turned me on—because of him. Because he was here, staring at me like he'd never seen anything sexier. Because he was touching me, tasting me.

Because he made me wait.

"I want to see you again. Want to see those pretty tits flush pink when you come."

A shudder ran through my body. My arms were boneless, useless, bound at my sides by their own sex-drenched laxity, and he used his free hand to unbutton my shirt. He pulled the cloth aside and tugged the bra down, all while steadily, slowly pumping his finger inside me. And then another, stretching me, giving me the faintest burn as my walls accommodated the extra width.

"What did I say I'd do to your nipples?"

"M-m-my nipples?" My voice was shaky, trembling. My whole body was trembling.

"That's right, baby. What am I going to do to them?"

"You're going to make them wet. With your mouth."

His dark gaze was approving. "That's when you come. When my lips are wrapped around your nipple, I want you to come on my hand. Understand?"

He didn't wait for my answer. His hand sped up, circling my clit, almost there, already painful. That was how he wanted it: painful. This was what he longed for, what he needed, what he gave in to sometimes. With a woman he paid, like me. Only not like me, because they usually came from an agency. Me, I'd gone through HR.

He leaned down, so close, and I almost came in

anticipation. But then he kissed the side of my breast instead. He worked lower, to the underside, grazing his teeth along tender, almost ticklish skin. And all the while his fingers worked me, bringing me higher, until my hips were rising to meet them, hungry and needy and so beyond shame now.

The urgency made me whimper, and he jolted at the sound. His mouth found my nipple, his lips closed around me. He'd given me permission to come when he did this. No, he'd given me an *order* to come, and I could have. With his fingers inside me and his thumb stroking my clit and his mouth at my breast, I could have come so hard. But it was the expression on his face that arrested me—at once tender and dark, both generous and cold.

My body shot into orgasm with all the power he used on me, the confident strokes of his fingers and the steady sucks of his mouth. I soared through my climax, seeing stars and blinking red lights and snowflakes falling, falling, coming back down to earth in a blanket of warm, white snow, but it wasn't the ground at all, it was his arms, and he was holding me, soothing me while I floated back into myself.

"What about you?" I mumbled.

"Shh."

I blinked rapidly, clearing my vision. "You really aren't going to come?"

"I can't," he said tightly. But I knew he could. He could slip inside me and come so easily. He could pump into my fist or my mouth. He just wouldn't do those things, because he was too afraid of hurting me. The irony was almost painful as he held me sweetly, believing the worst of himself while he treated me better than anyone ever had before.

CHAPTER SIX

ON THURSDAY MORNING the elevator dinged. I looked up to see the doors open. All of Mr. Thompson's appointments came through that elevator. It was the only way in or out. Sometimes they were men, all wearing suits and ties and nervous expressions. Other times they were women, and I had to wonder if he was *using* them the same way he'd used me. He left the door open a crack, so I knew he wasn't. Which just made me wonder *why* he'd left the door open. Did he know I'd wonder? Bottom line: I was slowly going insane.

This arrival was a man. Or a boy, really, younger than most of the execs who had appointments. He had pale blond hair and a grin that almost hid his unease.

He stopped in front of my desk. "Noah Waters. I'm here to see Mr. Thompson."

I double-checked the calendar in case there'd been any last-minute changes from when I'd memorized it at the start of the day. Despite the rocky start, or maybe because of it, I was determined to be freaking great at this job. And copier battles aside, I'd mostly managed it—even if all it had earned me were grunts and clipped thanks from the boss.

Your ten o'clock is here, I typed into the company IM system like Christy had taught me to do.

Mr. Thompson didn't immediately answer, so I figured he was on a call or something.

"He'll just be a minute," I told Noah with a nod toward the waiting chairs. The uncomfortable waiting chairs, which I'd found out one day when I'd sat in them. Had to be some kind of intimidation tactic, because the company could afford plush luxury on all the floors, especially the top. Not to mention my own chair behind the desk—Christy's chair—which was an ergonomic masterpiece.

But Noah didn't sit. "Are you new here?" he asked instead.

At my questioning look he gave me a sheepish smile. "I didn't see you at the Fourth of July picnic."

"Oh." I blushed. I wasn't sure *why* I blushed except there was something in his eyes that looked like interest. It had been a long time since I'd seen interest that didn't also come with a threat, like the guards in prison or strangers on the street. Or a certain billionaire just a few feet away. "I'm just temping until Christmas," I explained. "Nothing permanent."

He seemed disappointed but undeterred. "What's your name?"

"Angel. Christy will be back after the holidays. I'll be gone soon."

His smile finally faltered. "Me too, I think."

Sympathy tightened my lips. Dread and I were old

friends—old enough that I could recognize it in someone else. I wasn't sure I should ask but... "Is everything okay?"

"Okay? No, not really. It's a mess actually. A really big screwup."

Oh no. "I'm sorry. Maybe Mr. Thompson will understand. He's harsh but fair." I had slowly learned what Christy meant by that, watching Mr. Thompson in action. He was a lot of bark, but he only bit when it was really warranted.

Noah shook his head. "He won't understand this. Someone's going to take the fall, and it's going to be me."

The way he said it was full of conviction, as if he was determined to be the one. As if there might be someone else to do it.

Mr. Thompson's message appeared on my screen. *Send him in.*

"He's ready to see you now." I tried for a supportive expression—but I was pretty sure I failed. I'd seen exactly how the boss could be when he was pissed, and apparently he was pissed at Noah Waters. I had a feeling we were going to see the *Big Bad Billionaire* very soon, as if the white-winter sun outside was a moon, ready to turn the man into a monster. He would howl, and he would snap. I just hoped Noah would still be standing when Mr. Thompson turned back.

As Noah walked to the office and opened the door, another message popped up in the IM console. *Do the other assholes that work for me flirt with you?*

I stared at the message, shocked more by the tone of intimacy than the actual question. The tone of possession. It almost sounded like he was jealous. Which was ridiculous considering he'd touched me, he'd kissed my skin. He'd made me *come,* and then discarded me like it was all a big mistake.

It had been a mistake, I reminded myself. So where did he get off acting jealous?

I typed into the IM console. Noah was just being nice.

I glanced at the office, where the door was cracked open. I couldn't see inside, but I imagined Noah sitting in one of the chairs in front of the desk, waiting nervously for Mr. Thompson to acknowledge him. But Mr. Thompson must have been typing because a new message appeared.

Like I was nice to you?

I rolled my eyes. Sometimes smart people could be very stupid. Have a good meeting, I typed and shut the window.

Except it wasn't a good meeting. Over the next twenty minutes I listened through the opening in the door as Mr. Thompson blasted Noah for some mistake that had cost the company a lot of money. Based on the way Noah was defending himself—or rather, wasn't defending himself—it was a valid criticism. Still, I winced as Mr. Thompson's anger seemed to grow stronger with every passing minute.

And I couldn't help but wonder if I'd somehow made it worse by talking to Noah while we waited. Even though I knew I'd done nothing wrong.

"Pack your shit," I heard Mr. Thompson say. "And get out of my building."

My eyes widened. Without thinking out a plan, I was up from my seat. I crossed the short space and pushed the door open in time to see a defeated Noah standing up, his shoulders slumped and smile long gone.

"I'm sorry for disappointing you, sir," Noah said stiffly.

"Wait," I said. "You can't fire him."

Mr. Thompson sent me an icy glare. "What *are* you doing?"

Noah's eyes widened. Concern creased his forehead. "Yeah, Angel. What are you doing?"

Of course Mr. Thompson didn't miss the use of my first name. His eyes narrowed. And the truth was, I didn't know what I was doing. This was how I got myself into trouble, doing things without thinking them through. Leaving home because I knew I couldn't stay. Holding my boyfriend's boxes even though I knew they held illegal stuff, because he'd protected me on the streets. Lying on the job application because it was the only way I could work.

And now here I was, standing in front of the Big Bad Billionaire, probably about to lose my job for an entirely different reason. I licked my lips, fighting with myself. How the hell was I going to get out of this? But I was already neck-deep and sinking fast. "I'm just suggesting you rethink your position. Maybe he could find a way to fix his mistake at the beginning of the New Year."

"He lost the company over a million dollars."

My eyes widened. That was a lot of money. Still…
"It's a week before Christmas," I said weakly. "You can't
fire someone right before Christmas."

"Can," Mr. Thompson said. "Just did. It's called
making a point. In fact, I can do it again if you want
another demonstration?"

Oh shit, I couldn't be fired. Not when I'd done
everything right. *Except for keeping my mouth shut.*

"Angel," Noah said. "Don't get yourself in trouble
over me. It's not worth it."

"Listen to him," Mr. Thompson said. "He's really
not."

I narrowed my eyes. I may not be the brightest person in the room—definitely wasn't—but I knew how to
stand up for myself. In fact, getting picked on my whole
life had taught me not to back down. "Is that supposed
to impress me? The Big Bad Billionaire is going to blow
my house down?"

Noah sucked in a breath. "Angel."

Challenge sparked in Mr. Thompson's eyes, and I
almost thought… he *liked* when I talked to him this way.
Either that or he hated it, and he'd ruin my life and get
me thrown back in prison.

"No, I've got this," I said. "I'm not scared of him. All
my life people have tried to tell me to sit down and shut
up, but guess what? I'm not going to. You're firing
someone who doesn't deserve it, who's taking the fall,

and if I'm the only one with enough balls to say it to your face, then so be it."

Both men looked shocked. The tension was as thick as the snowstorm I could see through the window.

"Taking the fall," Mr. Thompson said quietly.

I took a deep breath—and a gamble. "Are you telling me that Noah was responsible for over a million dollars without a single safeguard in place? Without one other person checking his work? So where are they?"

"Mr. Waters?" Our boss drew out the name in a way that was somehow scarier than when he was yelling.

Noah shifted. "I told you I'm taking responsibility for this, and I am."

There was a long silence. Finally Mr. Thompson sighed. "I appreciate loyalty. I value it. But your loyalty needs to lie with the company. I need a *complete* report of what happened on this project. It's not just about protecting the people around you, especially since they didn't do the same for you. It's about making sure this doesn't happen again."

After a beat Noah nodded. "I'll tell you everything. But you need to understand, it was a culmination of mistakes that led to us losing that deal. And some of it was just plain bad luck. But I was the team lead, and I take responsibility for the outcome."

"Sit," Mr. Thompson said gruffly. Then he turned to me. His eyes narrowed. "And you. Outside. Now."

I scurried out of his office. Unfortunately that didn't provide much protection because Mr. Thompson followed me. *Damn it.*

Nerves ate me up from the inside like acid all through my body. My heart was pounding. I started babbling. "Look, I'm only here for one more week, but if you want me gone early—"

"Ms. Cole."

"Just so you know, I'd never even met Noah Waters before today and never plan to again, so it wasn't *anything* like flirting or—"

"Angel, listen to me. Part of the reason I was firing Mr. Waters was because I could tell he was holding back information about the project failure. I assumed he was covering his own ass. But we handle large-volume deals all the time. Losses happen. Mistakes happen."

"Oh."

"I don't go around firing my employees right before Christmas for making mistakes." He paused. "Or for speaking out of turn."

Relief coursed through me. "Cold but generous," I murmured.

His eyes darkened. "Don't make the mistake of thinking I'm a good man, Angel."

"Too late." The words came out a whisper.

He reached for me, his hand one inch from my face. I was sure he'd cup my cheek. Sure he'd lean down and kiss me, standing outside his office with Noah Waters waiting inside. And I wouldn't have turned away. I told him with my eyes just how much I wanted to feel his lips on mine. I didn't always do the smart thing. Almost never, in fact. I did what felt right, and this felt right. His eyes locked on mine, his hands on me. *He* felt right.

"You do something to me," he muttered. "I don't like it."

And just like that, a splash of cold regret doused any desire I had. Any hope. I may as well have rolled around in the snow for how I felt as he went into his office and shut the door.

I don't like it.

CHAPTER SEVEN

I CLOSED THE last of the files, satisfied that I'd finished my work before leaving. A bittersweet feeling because today was my last day.

It was also Christmas Eve, and most of the building had already left. At seven o' clock, it felt much later. Snowfall had grown heavier all day. It verged on a storm now, darkening the streets as people rushed to get home with last-minute packages. Lights were on in Mr. Thompson's office, and I knew he was still there, because he'd come in early this morning—and hadn't left yet.

I stared at the office door, which was cracked open. In invitation?

That was wishful thinking. I couldn't see inside, but maybe that was for the best. Even if I went in there, what would I say? He wouldn't care that I was leaving. For good, this time. I was just an awkward situation he'd be glad to get rid of.

But I cared. Tears sprang to my eyes, and I hated myself for being so transparent. How had I started to fall for my boss when I'd only worked here for two weeks? When the first time we'd met, he'd made me come so hard I couldn't breathe? When he watched me and listened to me and even flirted with me in that gruff, brutal way of his?

Okay, so maybe the crush wasn't that far-fetched considering.

Still, I shouldn't be thinking about saying anything else to him. Not even goodbye. I left a quick note for Christy letting her know the work I'd done, so she'd know where to pick up. Then I grabbed my purse and headed for the elevator.

I refused to look back at the office. Refused to care. I made it inside the elevator. The doors slid shut behind me... until a hand pushed in to stop them.

Mr. Thompson.

"Going down?" he asked.

I averted my eyes and nodded. Outwardly I remained calm and collected, but inside my senses went haywire like they did every time he was nearby. The size of him, filling up every spare inch in the elevator. The heat of him, making my skin tingle.

The musky male scent of him, turning me to liquid. *God, I need to get out of this elevator.*

Either that or I needed never to leave it.

Out of the corner of my eye I watched him step inside and press the button for the lobby. The elevator began moving.

"Do you have plans?" He cleared his throat. "For Christmas Eve?"

I blinked. Why was he making small talk after avoiding me for two weeks? And how embarrassing would it be to tell him no, I didn't have any plans?

I was saved from that embarrassment when the elevator shuddered to a stop, well before we would have reached the ground floor. The lights flickered and went off. I blinked as low yellow lights appeared from the bottom of the walls, giving me just enough illumination to make out the shadows.

The elevator doors didn't open.

"What's going on?" I whispered. Something about the darkness made it seem like I should be quiet.

He pressed the buttons, but they weren't even lit. "The storm must have taken down the grid."

Crap, just what I needed, to be trapped with the man I had an inappropriate and completely unrequited crush on. My heart began beating faster, as if this was some kind of private makeout session instead of just bad luck. "Security will know to look for us, won't they?"

"Yes." A beat passed. "Maybe not. There aren't many people with access to this elevator. And most people leave early on Christmas Eve. In fact, why are you still here?"

"I don't have any family in town." I didn't have any family at all, but he didn't need to know that. My daddy hadn't responded to my letter from jail, and maybe that was all I deserved after running away from home, for not trusting him enough to stay. *Stupid girl,* he'd called me.

Sometimes I thought running away had been the smartest thing I'd ever done.

"I see," Mr. Thompson said.

And I thought that, somehow, he may have figured it

out. Who spent the night before Christmas filing papers for a boss who didn't even like them? I did, apparently. Who stuck around at the end of a temp job because they didn't want it to be over? Me again.

Stupid girl.

I'd always believed I'd prove my dad wrong, but I never had, and days like this, I thought I never would.

Mr. Thompson pulled out his phone. Light from the screen filled the elevator with a blue glow, making it feel more intimate, more wrong. And more clear, as the faint light lit his face. "Damn," he muttered. "Signal is shit in here. Try yours?"

"I—I don't have a cellphone."

He glanced at me, and I felt his surprise overcome his frustration. "Why not?"

A blush heated my face. Thank goodness it was too dark for him to see the proof of my embarrassment. At least I hoped so. I certainly couldn't see the tan color of his skin or dark mahogany of his hair. He was all angles and shadows to me now, more a dream than reality, which made it easier somehow to tell the truth. "I can't afford one."

I expected him to look away. I *wanted* him to look away, to give me some relief, but instead his gaze sharpened even further. And I knew he was taking note of my clothes that didn't quite fit or the winter jacket with holes in it. "How long have you been working temp jobs?"

Oh God, was he going to find out now? At the very

end? It wouldn't matter if he fired me, but if he found out I'd lied and told the authorities, I could be put back in jail.

"This is my first job out of school," I said vaguely, desperately, hoping it would be enough.

"Have you applied for permanent positions?"

"Um. Yeah." I'd applied to a hundred positions, both permanent and not. Each time disclosing my criminal record. And then, when I'd gotten hungry enough and scared enough, I'd skipped the disclosure. And the HR person for Thompson Industries called me the next day. "Haven't found one yet."

"Why not?" The question was blunt. And painful.

"There are a lot of people looking for jobs. And not that many jobs. And, well, I'm not the brightest bulb. I know that too."

He made a dismissive sound. "That again."

"It's the truth," I said. *Liar.* "But I think I can do a good job. If I can find someone to take a chance on me."

Like you. But I didn't say that. All I was hoping for now was that he wouldn't ask any more questions. If I could make it out of this elevator, out of his sight, he'd forget all about the mousy temp assistant he'd had. And I'd be safe.

"I'm sure I'll find something soon," I said hastily, attempting a smile.

"Jesus," he muttered. Then without warning, he banged on the elevator doors. *Bang bang bang.* I jumped back, startled, my heart jumping into my throat.

The silence that followed rang in my ears. No footsteps came running. No shouts asked if we were okay.

No one was there.

I bit my lip. "Mr. Thompson?"

"I think, considering all that's happened, you can call me Gage," he said wryly.

My eyes lowered in the dark. "How long do you think it'll be?"

"Not long." A longer pause this time. "I don't know. There's always someone from security on standby even when the building is mostly empty. But they might be patrolling the grounds. They might be unable to get here due to the storm. For all I know, they could be in one of the elevator cars, stuck just like us."

"Oh."

With a muttered curse, he started pacing. Since the elevator car was small and his stride was long, he could only go one-and-a-half steps before turning. And with each turn, his movements got a little more jerky, his stride a little more clipped. He practically vibrated with tension; it filled the air, making me jittery and hot.

"Don't like small spaces?" I asked.

He turned to face me. "What?"

"Small spaces. They make you stressed? That's understandable."

He laughed shortly. "No, the space isn't the problem."

Was the problem... me? It seemed crazy that a girl like me could impact him this much, but clearly he was upset. Hurt arced through me. He'd already told me he didn't like me, didn't like the way I made him feel, but it still hurt to be reminded of it. "I'm sorry," I said, hating how my voice shook. "I'm sure they'll get us out soon."

He swore. "Don't look at me like that."

"You can't see me."

"That's where you're wrong, Angel. I can see you in the dark. I can see you with my eyes closed. I see you in my dreams. I can't seem to stop seeing you."

The air rushed out of me. "Mr. Thompson?"

"Don't *Mr. Thompson* me. You know exactly what effect you have on me with those goddamn ugly skirts and those goddamn ugly heels. And that smile. So fucking innocent. Do you practice that?"

Tears stung my eyes. "Why you talk like that to me?"

I waited for a sharp retort, something angry and cutting, but it never came. "Because I'm an asshole," he said shortly. "Because I don't know how to deal with you. With *this.*"

Pain laced his words, and my anger melted away. "You don't have to deal with me."

I won't be here tomorrow. Won't see you again. Am I the only one sad about that?

"I want you," he said, his voice raw and rough like an open nerve. "I *need* you. But I can't touch you."

Because of what he'd told me? It seemed impossible that it would hold him back if he really wanted something, wanted *someone,* and yet he seemed so torn. Like a wolf with his paw caught in a trap—except the trap wasn't a physical thing made of metal. The trap was his own past, his own mind. His own fears. My heart broke for the mother who'd seen her rape every time she'd looked at her child. It broke even more for the child who'd seen that shame in her eyes and understood he was the cause of it.

I can't touch you.

If he couldn't touch me, then I could touch him. I could be the bridge between us, my hand on his arm, his skin hot under my palm. His whole body stilled at the contact. I felt his muscles flex under my hand as a shiver ran through him.

"Don't do that." Almost a growl.

"Why not? You won't hurt me." To prove my point, I squeezed gently.

For a moment, his whole body leaned toward me. I was sure he would kiss me, but then he yanked himself away. "God, Angel. Do you want to be raped? Is that what this is about? Some sick game of chicken? Because I will do it. I'll hurt you, and I won't even feel sorry for it."

His words sickened me—not because I believed them, but because he did. He really believed he was capable of hurting me. I knew otherwise. And as for feeling sorry... he was already suffering deep, searing regret for things he hadn't even done, for crimes his father had committed.

"I'm not afraid of you," I whispered.

"Then you're an even bigger fool than you thought."

I winced. He'd said it to hurt me, and it had worked. For a moment, I turned away, facing the corner as I blinked back tears. But I knew how badly he wanted me, and that was enough to lend me courage. The courage to help him. Nothing I said would convince him. So I would have to show him instead.

With trembling fingers, I began unbuttoning my dress shirt, just like he'd done two weeks ago.

Despite the darkness, he noticed immediately. "What the hell are you doing?"

"Making a point," I said, repeating what he'd told me in the office that day with Noah Waters. I pulled my shirt from the waistband and faced him.

His breath caught. "Stop that right now."

I dropped the shirt on the floor and toed off my shoes. He backed up—but there was nowhere for him to go. His back hit the elevator wall, and he leaned back, pressing his head against the wall and staring at me through slitted eyes. His jaw must have been clamped shut the way the words came out. "I. Said. Stop."

"I heard you. But I'm not going to listen." I gave him an apologetic smile. "I stopped working at noon. It's Christmas Eve, you know."

"Not funny."

I reached behind me and unclasped my bra. I held it to my breasts as the straps fell down around my arms. "This isn't a joke."

"It's not going to be a joke when you're lying there, broken, hurt, because you didn't fucking take me seriously."

I didn't want my fingers to tremble as they worked at my skirt and my stockings, but I couldn't help it. Not with his threat hanging in the air.

"Angel," he said sharply.

I stilled, looking down. "What is it you like to do to girls?"

"Not girls, Angel. What I did before—that was scratching a fucking itch. What I want to do to you... is take you. Without a care for whether you like it or want it. Without making sure you can even *move* after that." He laughed shortly. "No, that's not true. The truth is I don't want you to be able to move. I want you fucking shattered underneath me. Understand?"

Oh, I understood. I understood that he thought he would hurt me, just like his father had hurt his mother. That he saw those impulses inside himself, the ones that wanted to pin me down and fuck me, and saw the pain and shame and hatred from his own conception. I understood that he saw the past repeating itself, and he cared enough about me to warn me away.

I couldn't bear the thought of him in pain, believing the worst of himself. Because he wasn't his father. He wasn't a rapist. And he wouldn't harm me, not really. I believed that—and I was about to stake my life on it.

I released my hold on the bra and let it fall to the ground.

He turned his head away as if the sight of my bare breasts—even in the shadows—was painful. Then he slid to the ground. "I don't want to hurt you," he muttered hoarsely.

"You won't," I promised him.

But he didn't believe me. Of course he didn't believe me; that was why I needed to prove it.

I sank to my knees in front of him. He started to reach for me... and then pulled his hands back. He reached up and grabbed the shiny metal bar that wrapped around the elevator walls. "I'm not going to touch you. You may be fucking suicidal, but I'm not going to help you do this."

A rough edge of fear marked his voice, and it hurt me to hear. But it also strengthened my resolve.

I put my hands on the bar beside his and leaned forward, my breasts right in front of his face.

"Oh God," he muttered and leaned forward, rubbing his face over my breasts, feeling them with his cheeks, his nose, his eyelids. Running the five o'clock shadow of his jaw over my tender flesh, abrading me. "So fucking beautiful."

He was lost in me, learning the shape of my breasts, breathing me in. And I was lost in him, gripping the bar tight through the pain, moaning softly when he caught one nipple in his mouth. He sucked, making it wet, just like he'd promised that first day, and my legs clenched together in response.

"Feels so good," I whispered. "Want more."

I knew my words were slurring as if I were drugged, and I *was*, high on the pleasure coursing through me, but he needed to know I was okay. It must have worked, because he did just what I asked. He licked and sucked and bit his way to my other nipple and sucked me there until I cried out.

He never released his grip on the bar.

I felt a little mean for teasing him this way, even though I hadn't meant it as a tease. I pulled back, and he groaned, sounding almost desperate. Then the sound changed, grew more urgent as I began unbuttoning his dress shirt.

"Wait," he gasped. "It's enough. Just let me... let me touch you again. Let me use you."

I knew exactly how good it would feel to let him do that, like he had the first day. And I knew it would end there, with me feeling wonderful and him still afraid of his own dark desires. I couldn't do that to him, even if he wanted me to.

Underneath his dress shirt was a white tank. I pushed it up out of the way, revealing the hard planes of his abs, his chest, lightly furred and clenched tight with restraint.

"So sexy," I murmured.

He laughed, unsteady—more an exhalation of air. "Angel, enough."

"No." I trailed a finger down his chest, enjoying the ripple of muscles, all the way down his abs and over his belt, to the bulge in his pants. It pulsed at my touch. "I don't think it's enough."

He made a muffled sound that I took as wholeheart-ed agreement. With him, that was as close as I would get.

I stroked him through his pants. "Keep holding on to the bar if you want."

"Okay." He shut his eyes. "I'm going to."

He said it like a threat. It made me smile. I was still smiling when I unzipped his pants and pulled out his cock. How pretty. He wouldn't like that word, but it was perfect for his cock. Long and thick and impossibly smooth. Already wet at the tip, because he wanted me that much. What could be prettier than that?

I leaned down and kissed the tip. He jerked in my hand. His whole body shuddered, but he didn't release the bar. When I pulled back, my lips were wet from his arousal.

"More?" I asked.

"I can't control it." He was pleading with me now. For me to keep going? Or for me to stop? Maybe both. Maybe he wanted to hurt me and have me forgive him.

I leaned down and closed my lips around the head of his cock.

"Fuck," he shouted. The word bounced off the walls, filling the elevator.

I used my hand to pump his cock while I sucked the head and swirled my tongue around. I tried to draw out every drop of salty precum, swallowing it down and searching out more. It was hard to take him deep in this position, with him sitting up straight. He was practically holding his body up, gripping the bar and pushing his hips toward me. I took him as far as I could, letting the wetness slide down and coat him, using it to lubricate my fist as I worked him.

"Sorry," he muttered. "Sorry, sorry, sorry."

I barely understood what he was saying, or why, until I saw his arms come down. As if released from a spring, they grabbed me before I could blink. He rocked forward, shoving me down to the floor, climbing on top of me. *Sorry, sorry, sorry.*

My breath was coming fast and then not at all. Was this it? Was he going to hurt me now, like he'd sworn he would? But I wasn't afraid of him. I was afraid *for* him. How much would he hate himself if he *did* hurt me? And I knew I would let him do anything to me. I'd never say no. Never make him regret anything we did together.

I let him move me, let him yank down my panties and spread my legs. Let him put his mouth against my sex, and God, God, it wasn't a hardship at all to let him suck my clit. He dipped low and slid his tongue into my folds, drawing out slickness and pleasure, making me shudder and cry out. Then he went high again, lashing my clit with steady, urgent strokes, begging me to come, demanding it.

"*Mr. Thompson.*"

His voice was muffled, but I heard him anyway. "God, yes. Again."

He pressed one finger inside me, working it along the inner walls until I clenched around him. He added another finger until I felt full—but not enough. Not even his wicked tongue on my clit or his deft fingers in my cunt were enough.

Tears fell down my cheeks. "Mr. Thompson," I whispered.

He lunged forward until his body canted over mine. His eyes were dark orbs above me, almost cruel. He notched his cock against my body, a warm and urgent threat. "I'm sorry, Angel."

Then he pushed inside me, relentless, giving me no time to adjust, no time to do anything but stretch and burn and ripple around his hard flesh as I sobbed his name. Immediately he pulled back and thrust inside me again, his pace faster than I could breathe, his movements so hard I felt like the whole elevator car was moving instead of just him.

It felt like his entire body was slamming into my clit, the friction too painful to come, but then he shifted position and his cock pressed a place inside me. I wrapped my legs around him and held on as he battered that place until I was begging him, asking for something with incoherent moans and stuttered breaths. Needing to come.

He pinned my arms above my head. "Angel. Oh fuck, Angel. I didn't want to hurt you."

I didn't have enough air to respond. I was barely holding on as he rode me. In the end it wasn't his cock filling me up or his hands on my wrists that made me come. It was his cheek brushing against mine that pushed me over, the unexpected intimacy of the moment, my heart swelling along with my clit as I shuddered beneath him.

My climax caused his, and he made a choked sound as he pressed himself into me, somehow deeper, somehow harder, straining against me while he filled me with his seed.

CHAPTER EIGHT

I GROANED. "OH God, that feels so good."

Gage's white smile was like the Cheshire cat's in the dark. "Too much?"

My toes scrunched up as he ran his capable hands over my heel. An extremely intimate sound escaped me. A footrub in a stalled elevator was officially the most decadent thing that had ever happened to me, and I never wanted it to end.

"Just right," I said on an exhale.

His voice grew serious. "You work too hard."

I had to laugh. "You're telling me that?"

"I own the company. I have a vested interest in its success. But you... you weren't even getting overtime. I checked."

Thank goodness it was dark so he couldn't see me blush. "I guess I thought if I did a good enough job, I might be considered for a permanent position."

Of course I'd known what a long shot that was, if only because it might require a more in-depth background check, one that might turn up sealed records.

But Mr. Thompson was silent, and I knew that he had never even considered offering me a permanent position. Not surprising, considering our first encounter, but it still hurt to know that he hadn't wanted me. I'd thought I did good work, but maybe I was wrong. Or maybe that didn't matter.

A few cards short of a deck, my daddy had said.

I tried to lighten the mood. "Not sure I'd want to work here anyway. What's with offices being so high and spacious? I'm more of a burrower."

"Angel…"

"Don't worry about it. I'll find another temp job. It's not a problem."

"Angel, I don't understand why you're trying to get a job like this. Filing papers? Filling out forms?"

"I don't know. I guess I just like paying my bills."

He barked a laugh. "Fair enough. I meant it isn't you. That isn't where your strengths lie."

"What strengths?" I wasn't fishing for compliments. I was genuinely curious if there was any way to earn a living while being both gullible and hopeless. Preferably not on my back.

"Angel, you're caring, you're courageous. You're also pretty damn smart no matter what you say. But as much as I'd love to see you every day, it'd be distracting to have you as my secretary. I don't think it would make you happy either, would it?"

"Well, I'd have food and clothes and maybe even my own apartment. They say money can't buy happiness, but those things make me pretty happy."

"You need to do *something*. You don't need to do

this. There are a lot of jobs in the world that aren't being an assistant to assholes like me."

"There aren't," I said flatly. "But I guess my daddy was right after all. I can't make it in the real world."

"This?" He made a sweeping gesture at the shiny metal walls of the elevator, at the marble floors. "This isn't the real world. This is a boxing ring, and you aren't going to be happy here because you don't like to hit people."

"I appreciate the attempt, but I know the real reason I'll never make it." And it wasn't even the criminal record I had to disclose on every job application. The real reason was what had gotten me in jail in the first place. Too trusting, too blind, and too...

He groaned. "Jesus. You need to stop with that. You're not stupid."

I gave him a look. Which probably would have been more effective if he could see my face. "Don't patronize me. I know what I am."

"Fuck, Angel. You of all people know me better than that. I'm not a nice person. I'm not going to tell you things just to make you feel better, not if I don't believe them."

That was true, he wouldn't.

"Who told you that?" he demanded. "Your father? If so, he's an asshole."

Something shifted inside me to have Mr. Thompson acknowledge that. Because my daddy had been an asshole. He hadn't cared when they'd diagnosed me with some kind of learning disability, and he definitely hadn't gotten me the help they'd recommended. No, he'd been too interested in me for all the wrong reasons, kissing and hugging me while he insulted me, hoping I was too stupid to figure out why he really liked to hold his thirteen-year-old daughter so close. I'd learned to keep my head down. Learned to stay under the radar.

Learned to be stupid, so no one would ever pay attention to me.

Or maybe I was just fooling myself. Maybe I was just stupid and desperate enough to make up reasons.

A cold sensation wrapped around me, gripping me with its fingers and squeezing tight. There were no more reasons to make up. No more excuses. "You don't know what you're talking about," I said flatly.

He blinked, clearly not used to people talking to him that way. But he didn't get angry. Instead his eyes softened. "I know you're smart in everything that matters. You're smart about people. You're smart about the way I treat you and the way you treat me." He paused. "You're smart about us."

About us. Oh God. I wanted there to be an us. And how stupid was that? "I have a record," I whispered.

"What?"

"I have…" Damn it, this was harder than I'd thought. And I'd thought it would be pretty freaking hard. "I have a criminal record, okay? I got out of jail six weeks ago. I was inside for two years, for conspiracy to possess with intent to distribute."

He stared at me, mouth open. His brown eyes were no longer angry or fierce. They were shocked, and for the first time I noticed his dark lashes. They made him seem younger, almost vulnerable. He was like the building, hard steel and concrete—and the thin layer of glass that I'd slammed into like a sledgehammer, breaking it with no care at all, only concerned about what this job would mean to me.

He shook his head slowly, disbelieving. "You were… a drug dealer?"

A short bitter laugh escaped me. "That would require some level of intelligence. And in that case, I wouldn't be broke. No, I was just the dumb girlfriend of the dealer. I kept the boxes in the room I was renting because he'd asked me to. And when the cops showed up to search them…"

"Jesus, Angel."

"I do have my diploma," I said somewhat defensively. "At least that part was true. I got my associates degree while I was there. But I didn't disclose my crime on the application. That's the only reason I got this temp job."

He was silent a moment, the darkness almost suffocating as I waited for him to judge me. He couldn't say anything worse than I'd already told myself. But it would still hurt, from him.

"How the *fuck* does a minor get two years in prison for someone else's crime?"

Surprise held me suspended, almost floating above the cool elevator floor, hanging by a breath. He didn't seem mad… at me. It had to be a mistake. A temporary reprieve. Just one more thing I didn't deserve. "The judge said I needed to learn my lesson. That running away from home had proven how little responsibility I took for my life. He said that even if I hadn't meant to, I should have known better."

"That's ridiculous. What was his name?"

"The judge?" My eyes widened. What did he want to know that for? "I'm not telling you."

"I'll find out easily enough."

"It's sealed. My record is sealed. The judge did that much for me, at least."

My heart seemed tight, my chest too small to contain it. I found myself clutching the elevator floor, almost bracing myself for whatever would come next. Whatever he would say, whatever he would do—except before he could say anything, footsteps approached from… above? Through the door, but it almost sounded like the floor was halfway up.

Gage was on his feet in a flash. "Hello," he shouted. "Anyone there?"

Someone shouted back. "I hear you. You okay in there?"

That almost sounded like the man out front…except I didn't know his name. "Santa?" I called, feeling silly.

There was a laugh. "Yes, ma'am. I knew you went in this morning and never came out. Figured I better check on you."

I smiled. "Thank you. We could use your help."

"Call security." The Big Bad Billionaire was back. "Tell them Mr. Thompson is in elevator bank three and to get their asses down here."

"Will do."

It got quiet, and Mr. Thompson sent me a sideways glance. "How do you suppose he got in with the doors locked?"

He must have found some way in, maybe a way that wasn't totally kosher, but I wasn't going to complain about that. Or let him get in trouble. It was my last day, and even if it hadn't been, I'd have been fired after that confession. "The chimney, of course."

CHAPTER NINE

AFTER ADJUSTING A strand of glittery tinsel, I stepped back to examine my work. The little household plant bore its Christmas trappings with dignity… kind of like a dog forced to wear a Halloween costume. Well, a Christmas tree wouldn't fit in my room here. Not that I'd been able to afford one.

I dropped onto my couch and sat back. Maise wandered over and curled up on my lap. I stroked her absently. "It's nice, isn't it?"

Maise purred.

"Just don't eat the tinsel. I'm pretty sure it won't digest well."

A knock came at the door. I frowned. The owner of the house had gone to visit her son in Alabama. I was watching Maise until she got back, though to be honest, the gray and white striped cat had taken up residence almost since I'd gotten here. There were a few other people living in the house, but they were at work.

Which meant I had no idea who was knocking on the door.

I pushed a reluctant Maise off my lap and went to peer through the peephole. Oh God. "Mr. Thompson?"

"Gage," he said.

My heart started beating like crazy. What was he doing here?

Was he finally going to turn me in?

He looked about cold enough to do it, his mouth set in grim lines. In fact his face seemed starker than it had been, shadows under his eyes and a shadow of scruff on his hard jaw.

And deep inside, stupid hope beat against my ribs, clamoring to get out, and God, I didn't want to be wrong. Not again. Not about this. I needed some kind of protection around my heart, but seeing him standing outside my door in that ratty hallway tore down every defense I might have had.

"It's Christmas," I said, stalling.

"That's why I came today," he called. "I knew you couldn't turn me away on Christmas."

Damn him, he was right. Just like I'd told him he couldn't fire a guy a week before Christmas. Fear and a small, strange excitement warred inside me as I opened the door a crack.

His expression was reserved. He held up a small box wrapped in red and gold. "I come bearing gifts. Well, one gift."

If there were handcuffs in there, I was ready to be seriously pissed. Well, unless he had a different use planned for them... But worrying would get me nowhere. I had no choice but to open the door and show him up to my room. Then close the door and take his coat, as if he would be staying awhile. Doing anything else was physically impossible.

"I didn't take you for a cat person," he said as Maise twined between his legs.

"She's not mine." Just to be contrary I said, "But she's sweet. I could've had a cat."

"I see you with a dog. Something small but energetic."

I'd have done anything for a dog. Only, even as a young girl I'd been smart enough not to ask for things. Maybe I hadn't always been stupid. I'd just spent my brain cells on survival, on staying under my daddy's radar so he'd never have leverage against me. Never touch me. "I'm not allowed to keep pets here anyway. Maise belongs to the owner of the house."

He wandered farther into the room. He stooped to examine my pathetic houseplant Christmas tree. I felt overexposed with him seeing where I lived. How I lived. He looked sharp in a suit—even outside of work, on Christmas day. That was him, covered in masculine linen and silk, wrapped like a present.

"I'm starting a new trend," I said lightly.

When he glanced back at me, his expression was solemn. He looked less like a stranger, more like the Gage Thompson I knew from the office. The Big Bad Billionaire... but even with his stern face, I wasn't intimidated by him anymore. If he wanted to ruin me, it would be only too easy. With his money and his power, he could ruin anyone. I was completely at his mercy, and

I found, for some reason, that I liked it here. It didn't feel scary.

It felt safe.

I didn't think he was here to turn me in. "Did you come to offer me a job?"

He glanced at me sideways. "Do you want one?"

"Depends what I'd have to do."

A small smile turned his lips, challenging and intimate. "What if I said you had to come to my office, late at night when no one else is there?"

My stomach knotted. "I'd say that sounds familiar."

He withdrew something from his pocket. Folded paper that he opened. "Angel Marie Cole," he read.

My heart sank. "What is that?"

But I knew. I knew what it was even before he said, "Your job application. And let me tell you, this wasn't easy to get on Christmas Eve at midnight."

"You own the company."

"And as such, I'm considering a complete overhaul of our filing system. It took me two hours to find this."

Despite my distress, a smile tugged at my lips. He hadn't wanted to disturb his employees on Christmas Eve, in the middle of the night, so he'd done it himself. I imagined him bumping into file cabinets, swearing under his breath, and thumbing through stacks of files.

But no matter how adorable the image was, it didn't change what was on that paper.

Anger rose up in me, which was a whole lot easier than dealing with the truth. I didn't like him being disappointed in me. Didn't like being disappointed in myself. "You had no right to pull that out."

He gave me a dark look. "I had every right."

"You can't fire me. I'm not your employee anymore."

His expression softened. "And why would I fire you?"

I stared at him. "Because I lied."

"Angel… your juvenile record was sealed. That's why we didn't find it during the background check. And that means you don't have to disclose it."

My gaze narrowed. "What?"

And more importantly, how the hell did he know that?

The question must have shone in my eyes because he gave me a half smile. "I do numbers for a living. I could work out the dates here between your birthday, your GED, and your associates degree. And the date you submitted this application."

That much made sense, but… "How do you know about not having to disclose juvenile records?"

"I'm a business owner," he said lightly as if his business wasn't a billion-dollar conglomerate. "It's my responsibility to understand basic hiring laws." His cheeks darkened. "Plus I may have called my lawyer to confirm that this morning."

Blood had started to pound thickly in my ears. I felt close to crying, and that somehow seemed the worst travesty of this whole thing—crying in front of the man I wanted, the one I'd never deserve to have. "Why didn't I know about that?"

"You should have. Your parole officer should have gone over all this."

I just shook my head, remembering the flyer of homeless shelters and the offer to make money on my back. I'd known then that it wasn't how things were supposed to be done, but a lot of rules got broken in prison. And not all of them by the inmates.

He stepped forward, his finger raising my chin. "You don't have to worry anymore."

Worry? I had plenty to worry about. He didn't understand that in his thousand-dollar suit and his supreme self-assurance.

I shook my head. "I can't even blame my criminal record. It's not like I was so freaking successful before I got arrested. The truth is, I can't cut it, okay?"

"Never going to cut it?"

Why was he making me spell this out? God, it was so obvious. And so depressing. "I'm never going to make a bunch of money, got it? Never going to be one of those fancy people in a business suit. Never going to take the elevator to the top of the glass building."

"Well, we can't all be Willy Wonka."

Don't smile, you'll only encourage him. But I couldn't help it. I was glad he'd told me about the disclosure thing, and a deep sense of relief filled me. It meant I hadn't broken any rules getting that temp job. It also meant I could probably find another job, without a criminal history—and possibly with a positive recommendation. "You are such an asshole."

Or maybe without the recommendation.

He didn't seem bothered. "I've heard that before."

"Well, I'm not very original."

"Do not start with the smart stuff again. You're smart." When I snorted, he pressed on. "Very smart. The smartest woman I've ever met."

I glared at him. "Stop."

"It's true," he insisted. "I wish I had half your skill with people. I generally have to take over someone's company to get them to listen to me. Sometimes it feels like overkill."

"Only sometimes?" I asked wryly.

"But you, you just smile in that open way and say something sweet, and people are eating out of the palm of your hand." Something fell, then, in his eyes—a wall. A barrier. He took it down and let me see the truth of his words. "It worked for me, anyway."

My chest felt tight. "Not smart enough to get a job. The real kind. Not pouring stale coffee."

"You had a rough start," he countered. "You *survived* on the streets. And now look at you. Do you think I don't know how far you've come? Do you think I don't realize how hard you had to work to get to this point without a family, without a home?"

Yeah, kinda. "You're rich."

His expression softened. "I wasn't always rich. But you're right. I was never homeless either. So let me help you."

"What?"

"Let me give you money," he said bluntly.

Ah, there was the Big Bad. It was almost comforting that he wouldn't be cheesy or romantic about this. He was giving it to me straight.

"I'm not visiting your office, Gage. Not at night. Not at any time of the day."

"That's not what I'm asking for. I seem to recall you telling me I deserve more. That's what I want. From you. I want you with me when I go home. I want a reason to actually go home."

"And I'd be what? Your kept woman? Your mistress?"

"I was thinking girlfriend."

I fought against the wave of inappropriate happiness inside me. "This isn't right. The money. The imbalance. It's like you paying a woman to come to your office. That's not how it's supposed to work."

He took my hands and pulled me close. "Angel... I want to be with you. Near you. Is that wrong?"

I should pull away. I really should. And I would just as soon as I leaned in close and soaked up all his warmth. "No, you know that isn't wrong. I want that too."

"And I want you to have food," he continued in that persuasive tone of his. I imagined him using that tone when negotiating a multimillion-dollar deal, and felt strangely flattered by the comparison. "I want you to have clothes and your own apartment. Is that wrong?"

"No..." I drew the word out.

"And I want you to be happy." He pulled me flush against his body, his mouth against my temple. "So let me buy you a little happiness," he whispered.

I bit my lip to stop the laugh, but it came out anyway. "I did set myself up for that one."

"You can figure out your next step. You can try out different jobs. You can do whatever the fuck you want, but do it near me. That's all I want." He looked down at me, his eyes dark and somehow bright. "That's my happiness."

I swallowed thickly. "Oh, Gage."

His expression was tight, almost pained in its uncertainty. This wasn't a man used to uncertainty. "Is that a yes? Will you let me make you happy? Will you be mine?"

"It's a yes, please."

And he was good to his word, giving me the happiness I needed and wanted, bending his head to brush his lips across mine, deepening the kiss until I was lax in his arms and he was breathing heavy with need. One of his hands was threaded through my hair, cradling my head as he delved his tongue into my mouth. His other hand roamed my body from my breasts, down my stomach, to cup my ass, and then started the trek all over again— with a kind of urgency born of denial, as if he thought he'd never get to touch me again and had to prove to himself that he could.

When he pulled back, his eyes were hazy with desire. They focused on me with slow-burning intensity. "Show me your bedroom, Angel."

"Why?" I looked up at him, coy. "Do you have something to show me?"

"I have several things to show you," he growled. "Right here on the floor if you don't take me to your bed."

Ooh, I liked him growly. "Wait. First I need to see what's in the box."

He raised an eyebrow. "Mercenary. I approve."

I shrugged, unapologetic. I was way too curious about what he'd gotten. Besides, it had been a long time since anyone had given me a present. As soon as he handed me the box, I pulled aside the ribbon and tore the paper. Lifting the lid, I found a gleaming onyx pen inside. His pen. I picked it up, admiring the smooth shine.

Only then did I notice the engraving along the side. *Property of the Big Bad Billionaire. Please return if found.*

My jaw dropped. This was exactly how he'd gotten his reputation. And just like the man in the Santa costume had said, he lived up to his reputation. "Oh, you're very bad."

"So they tell me. Big too."

I swatted him. "Arrogant, overconfident, egotistical—"

"But you didn't think I meant… *you*, did you? Only the pen is mine. That's what I meant."

"I see," I said, even though he was such a tease. A sexy tease, and I never wanted him to change.

I loved him like this—demanding and confident like he should be, none of the hesitation and self-disgust he'd had before. Sometimes we were the worst judges of ourselves. He wasn't a rapist, no matter what his father had done. And I wasn't stupid, no matter what my daddy had said.

"But you can use it. Now that you're my girlfriend, I don't want you going around, borrowing other men's pens."

"Not when you have a perfectly good one."

He leaned down and kissed me, murmuring between hot presses of his mouth on mine, "Perfectly. Good."

I wrapped my arms around his neck and held on tight for what I was sure would be rough and wild and absolutely decadent. My lips close to his ear, I whispered, "You're too pretty, and it's been too long."

His lips curved against my neck as he recognized the same words he'd spoken to me. "Do you know what you're asking for?"

Better than he did, almost. And I wasn't afraid.

CHAPTER TEN

H E DIDN'T REACH for me right away. Didn't pull me close or pin me down. Not yet.

Instead his gaze was appraising, weighing my sincerity. Wondering whether I could take him. I raised my chin. I'd survived on the streets. Survived prison. If there was anyone strong enough to survive him, it was me.

"It's too late to back out now," he warned.

"Use me," I said softly. "I won't break."

He cocked his head. His gaze took me in, from my nipples pebbling underneath my threadbare cami to my bare feet, visible beneath the hem of my too-long pajama bottoms. Not exactly the sexiest outfit, but the hunger in his eyes left no doubt that he wanted me. And I knew exactly how he wanted me: hard. Rough. And fighting back.

"Will you tell me if I go too far?" he asked, almost conversationally, in the same tone he might use to wonder if we'd have a white Christmas. *Will it snow?* he'd ask. *Will I know when I break you?* he'd wonder. *After the fact, when it's too late to matter.*

Being with him was putting my trust in him. "You won't."

He shut his eyes. He could handle touching me, holding me, pounding me, but the trust was too much. And just right. When his eyes opened again, they glinted with lust—and hard steel. "Then we'll pick up where we left off."

And I knew he didn't mean after in the elevator, with my lips around his hot, pulsing flesh or my legs spread wide for him. He meant before that. He meant the very beginning, in his office.

My voice came out small and somehow more confident than I'd ever felt. "You were making me come."

"That's right," he said, approving, the same way he'd tell me I'd turned in the reports on time or followed his directions exactly. The tone of command and condescension sent a wash of humiliation through me—quickly followed by arousal. This man was power. He was threat and generosity wrapped into one sleek package, and I wanted more. I'd never get enough.

"Turn around." His voice was rougher now. Colder.

I turned willingly, nerves fluttering in my stomach, a tight knot lodged in my throat. Tonight was a test, whether he meant it that way or not. He'd either bend or break me, and if he did the latter, I feared for him more than myself. He'd never forgive himself if he hurt me, which was why I needed to be strong.

I reached to flip off the lamp. A brush of air was my only warning before hands gripped my hips. He pulled me back, pressing my ass flush against his body, his erection an iron bar, threatening and hot even through our clothes.

The soft fabric of my cami gave way to his rough hands, slipping under my breasts and plumping them up.

He groaned, looking down. "The first time I saw these."

His hands seemed large or my breasts seemed small. His hands tanned and rough against my pale skin. In every way he was stronger, darker, more powerful. I shivered, overpowered and subdued before I'd even thought to fight back.

"What did you think?" I asked, imagining that night when he'd thought he was a prostitute. And he wasn't that far wrong. I'd been desperate then—to keep the job, to survive. Desperate to please him, the same way I felt now. The same but different, because this time I knew I could say no.

"I thought you were more beautiful than I had any right to. And I felt better that I was paying you, because at least then you'd be getting something in return."

"I'm getting something. I'm getting you."

A low laugh. "We'll see if you still think that when I'm through with you. When I've bruised and bitten your pretty little tits. When you think you can't take it in any deeper or harder, but I force you to."

My inner muscles clenched, preparing myself and wanting at the same time. I could have told him I wasn't afraid, but we were beyond that, into the place where he threatened me because it turned me on—and because it turned me on too. He didn't need my reassurance; he needed my fear, and my body responded with obedience, sending my blood racing through my veins, my breath coming fast.

"What else?"

"Do you want to know what I'm going to do to you? I'm going to bend you over this bed, with my hand on your back to keep you down. Then I'm going to slide into that hot, wet heat of yours and get myself off with the friction of your cunt."

I moaned, afraid and hungry. "Wait," I said uselessly.

He didn't wait. When I tried to stand, but his hand touched my lower back, holding me down, bent over.

Exactly like he'd said he would.

My hands braced on the bed, but it wasn't enough. Not when he shoved a hand underneath my cami and squeezed—not a careful caress like he'd done before. He squeezed my soft flesh until an anguished cry left my lips, and then he didn't let up. He found the nipple between his thumb and forefinger and pressed, deliberate and cruel.

"Like this," he muttered, and I wasn't sure if the question was meant for me or himself.

But then he pressed harder, and a whimper escaped me. "No," I whispered.

That seemed to be what he wanted, because he started to move then, using my breasts like handles, pulling me back onto his cock, jerking himself off with the softness of my ass. Breathy, pained sounds filled the air around me, and I realized I was making them—almost a song, a sick kind of rhythm.

A large hand reached around and cupped my sex. "It will hurt more if you're dry," he said, his voice low and more menacing for how calm he sounded. Like he wanted me to hurt.

My clit pulsed at the warmth of him, desperate for more. I didn't think dryness would be a problem—not with the way my body was already responding to him, slick and hot. But he could still hurt me.

He probably would.

I ground my clit down on his palm, seeking him, and he groaned. "You don't care what I do to you, is that it? You get off on the pain, don't you?"

I flinched, because I hadn't been expecting him to call me out on it. I should have, though. I should have known he'd want to hurt me and make me want it and make me feel humiliated for it too. Should have known he'd wring every last drop of sensual torture from our play, or he wouldn't really be Gage Thompson.

The female body was made to be invaded, made to be entered, but he fanned his fingers over my sex and then squeezed, making me feel small and owned and *fucked* without even slipping his fingers inside me. My muscles clenched around nothing, aching, bruised and needy. "God, don't," I moaned. "*Please.*"

"It's really too late for that," he said in his cool, calm CEO tones. The same tones he'd used telling Noah he was fired. "Give me your hands."

My hands were the only things holding me up off

this bed. If I gave them to him, I would have no leverage left, no protection. No control. And that was exactly the way he wanted me.

I reached back, and he clasped my wrists together, deft and sure. And just as quickly released me. I only had seconds to register my freedom before he took it back, reaching around me, grasping my cami—and oh God, pulling, yanking it. A strap tore. The sound ripped through the air. And then the ruined fabric was pulled back, wrapped around my wrists, holding me effectively, leaving his hands free to touch and roam and pinch.

A cry filled my throat, low and desperate.

He laughed softly. "So pretty. This is how I imagined you that night, when I saw you bent over my desk." His lips found my ear, and he traced them along the curve. His voice came soft, then—I had to strain to hear. "And now I have you."

"Please," I whispered. But I didn't just want his dark words, his harsh promises. I wanted him to touch me, to force me. I even wanted him to hurt me, as long as he took care of me too. Those steel bars had kept me imprisoned—and they'd kept me safe. He was steel, and he would hold me, keep me. He'd protect me.

He pulled back and pushed down my pants. Cool air washed over the backs of my legs. His fingers skated up my thigh, teasing the hem of my panties. I squirmed, aching for more, harder, now, but he held me still. He held me with his hands and my bunched up cami. With a single muttered word: "Stay."

I stayed. I stayed while he hooked his fingers into my panties and dragged them down my legs. He pulled them taut around my ankles, spreading my legs just far enough to hold them there.

He was silent, but I felt his gaze like a touch. On my pussy, on my legs. On my ass. He watched me with total patience—the kind of patience that came with possession. There was no hurry, because he knew he'd have me for as long as he wanted. Because he knew he'd have me for a long time.

The first touch between my legs wasn't from his hands. He kissed me. He pushed his face between my thighs, shoving them apart until I bent my knees. He licked and sucked at my pussy, only reaching the outer lips. Every nip and suck made me push back harder against his face, aching for more.

"God, I can't—" My fingers grasped at nothing, at air.

"You can," he said, returning to his torment. When he finally added a finger, it only got worse. And so much better, the sweet stretch of him, the brutal rhythm.

I choked on my next refusal when he stood. A zipper running down. A rustle of clothing. A tear of foil. My whole body tensed, ready for him, waiting.

He notched his cock against my opening, hot and blunt where I was slick.

Then he was inside me, shoving all the way in before I'd had a chance to breathe, too fast for me to even cry out. He impaled me, and I shuddered in a kind of sensual shock, pinned down by him, laid bare. There was nothing to do but take it, nothing to hold on to, no gravity at all except the hard, implacable length of him pushing me down on the bed.

It was exactly what he'd threatened—what he'd promised—and exactly what I needed. I need to know that he would be there, keeping his word, hurting me and protecting me. I needed to know, when I was alone in the world, when it was Christmas Eve, that someone wanted me enough to take me.

"This." His voice was choppy, breathing rough. I wasn't the only one breaking apart. Wasn't the only one crashing. "This is what I imagined doing. Fucking you until you couldn't breathe. That's what I want."

And he'd gotten it, because God, I couldn't. Couldn't breathe, couldn't think. My body was a mass of burning sensation, like the sun. I was heated from the inside and melting on the surface. It hurt to look at anything, blinding, so I shut my eyes tight. But the light found me there, flares of red and electric white light. I couldn't escape the burn. It consumed me, flames licking at my skin, molten deep in my core, the temperature rising until I came, calling his name, *Gage,* clenching around him, feeling his body tense behind me as he growled out his climax.

We remained like that, me bent over the bed, him collapsed on top of me, my muscles pulsing around him, his flexing inside me, our bodies communing while our breaths slowed down. When he finally moved and his cock slipped from inside me, I felt the loss acutely, the space he had filled now empty.

He found another way to fill it, with firm and gentle touches, moving my body onto the bed, settling me under the covers before he disappeared into the bathroom for a few minutes. When he came back, he had a warm washcloth that he used on me, soothing the secret places on my body, tender spots he had used roughly, bruises he had left.

My limbs were limp as he arranged me, moved my legs apart to give him access, and then slid them closed again. In all that we'd done, this was the first time I'd gotten a clear view of his body, the sinewy muscle and dark hair. Carefully banked power treating me gently.

And then he was behind me, pulling me against his chest. I was helpless against his warmth and so damn sated. And half-asleep when we heard the city clock chime twelve times.

"Merry Christmas, Angel," he murmured.

"Merry Christmas," I whispered back.

The rumors hadn't lied. He was big and he was bad, but he was mine. And I was his.

THE END

THANK YOU!

Thank you for reading *His for Christmas*! I hope you enjoyed Gage and Angel's story.

- Would you like to know when our next books are available? You can sign up for my newsletter at skyewarren.com/newsletter.

- Like me on Facebook at facebook.com/skyewarren.

- I appreciate your help in spreading the word, including telling a friend.

- Reviews help readers find books! Leave a review on your favorite book site.

- His for Christmas is one of my sweet books—sexy and romantic and sometimes serious, but without any dark captivity. If you enjoyed this story, you may also enjoy my Beauty series. Turn the page to read an excerpt from that story...

Beauty Touched the Beast

Erin cleans Mr. Morris's house twice a week, soaking up every moment with the reclusive ex-soldier she secretly loves. Blake Morris knows he's scarred both inside and out and is no good for the beautiful young woman who cleans his house to pay for college. But when Erin walks in on Blake touching himself and moaning her name, all bets are off.

"I love this "Beauty and the Beast" story that Skye Warren has crafted. She puts a twist to this classic tale that makes it different and deliciously erotic."

—Nina's Literary Escape

"I consider this series a Top Pick because their story is not only very memorable and extremely sexy, but I could read this series many times over and never tire of it. In fact, I already know I will revisit them again for years to come."

—Ms Romantic Reads

EXCERPT FROM
BEAUTY TOUCHED THE BEAST

E RIN JOGGED UP the steps of the farm-style house in good spirits.

She let herself in using her key and called out, "Mr. Morris! It's Erin."

Call me Blake, he always asked, but for some reason she resisted. She wasn't usually a stickler for propriety, but with him it seemed like a good idea. Maybe his military roots made the formality more correct to her. Or more likely, it was the domesticity of cleaning his home while he loitered near her.

It would be so easy to slip, to let him see how she felt about him. Then she'd feel like an idiot—a dumb, little girl panting after a man old enough to be her father.

She pulled a book from her bag and went upstairs in search of her boss to return it to him. She could probably put it in his bookcase, always neat and organized so she'd know right where it belonged. In fact, his whole house sparkled from the knotted floorboards to the arched ceilings.

It was partly because he was so fastidious, but also because she did a full deep clean twice a week. It was one of the odd habits that made her reclusive employer so strange, and also endearing.

She could replace the book, but she wanted an excuse to talk to him. They'd had a lively debate on the merits of the U.N. in her political science class yesterday and she knew he'd appreciate it.

She poked her head in his bedroom and found him there. Her breath caught in her throat as she took in the sight. He lay spread out on the bed, his skin still damp from a bath, a towel in disarray around his waist.

And he was masturbating. *Shit!*

She ought to leave. This was clearly a private moment and she the intruder. She really should turn around, walk away and absolutely, positively not watch. Instead she stood there, her eyes riveted to his exposed cock standing up thick from his fisted hand.

"God, baby," he moaned, his eyes closed, "Suck it, please."

Her lips parted in surprise, as if she could obey him from across the room. Her clit throbbed to hear his rasping voice say those dirty words, to watch his fist fuck his cock.

"Yes. *Yesss.* So beautiful. God." His other hand reached to cup his balls. "That's right, baby. Lick them. Suck them."

Her wide-eyed gaze flew to his face, mesmerized by the interplay of shiny, scar tissue and ruddy, healthy skin twisted in a grimace of pleasure. His burns and coarse features might make him repulsive to some, but when she looked at him she saw only Blake, with his brilliant ideas and gruff kindness.

"Touch yourself. Yeah, yeah. Take me deep in your mouth and stick your fingers in your cunt."

Her thighs squeezed together where she stood, giving herself whatever relief she could. If she moved, either her legs or her hands, she'd have to acknowledge that what she was doing, that being a voyeur was wrong, so she stayed still instead.

Then, shockingly, he moaned her name, "Erin…"

Erin barely had time to process that, and then he came, spurting into his cupped hand.

More than a little turned on, she let out an involuntary sound—a whimper, almost. Heavy lids slid open as he turned to look at her. His eyes widening into a look of shock, even horror.

Mortified, she turned and ran down the stairs. The sound of her name hurtled down the steps after her, not in passion this time, but she couldn't go back.

Pacing in the kitchen, she battled her embarrassment at being caught in a compromising position. Or rather, she'd caught *him* in a compromising position. But since it was his house, and she just cleaned it for him, she'd messed up big time. She'd have to face him and apologize, but she couldn't look for him in his bedroom. Not right then and maybe not ever.

Her hands caught on the stone edge of the countertops, then flitted across the surface. Already clean, as usual. She'd never done anything quite this embarrassing. Watching the man's private moment? That was low. And even worse, she respected him, so much. She *liked* him, and she might have ruined everything.

She pulled out the cleaning supplies, thinking that at least she could subvert her nervous energy into something useful. She'd come here to clean, not to moon after Blake and certainly not be a peeping Tom.

Blake bounded down the stairs soon after, wearing his customary sweats. She'd admired him before, the way the loose, comfortable clothing hung on his well-built shoulders and abs, but now all she could see was his naked, damp body. As if she hadn't already proven herself enough of a coward, she turned away as if to flee.

"Erin," he said in those low tones that always made her clench. "Wait, please."

She paused and turned halfway back to him, willing the inappropriate, private, *sexy* images to subside. A reddened cock. Thick ropes of come. *Dammit.*

"I'm sorry you had to see that," he said. "Don't … quit. It won't happen again. Please," he said.

She'd never expected to see him like this, practically begging—not for anything, and certainly not for his maid to continue cleaning for him. Did she really vacuum so well?

But no, if nothing else, today had shown that he at least *thought* about her in another way. Is *that* why he kept her around, why he increased her cleaning schedule and chatted with her about his work? Should she be offended?

But she wasn't. She was flattered. And turned on as hell.

She stammered, "I don't understand. Were you…was I…?"

He closed his eyes and lowered his head. "There's no excuse," he said, swallowing. "But I won't—" He broke off and looked away. The part of his face turned toward her was the more scarred half. That gesture more than anything showed his distress since he usually took pains to hide it when possible.

"What can I do so that you will not leave?" he asked.

"I—honestly, I hadn't even thought of that. Actually, I wanted to apologize. For intruding on your privacy. I'm not going to quit."

"Thank you," he said stiffly, either in acknowledgement of her apology or her agreement she didn't know. He paused then repeated, "I'm sorry." After a curt nod, he disappeared into his study.

She thought maybe she should have told him that he didn't have anything to be sorry for, that he hadn't done anything wrong, after all. But it would be too strange to correct him in his assumption. What could she say? *Please, go ahead and use me in your fantasies. I don't mind.* That would hardly make this situation less awkward.

Besides, she needed time to think, to process what she had seen him do and her feelings. But she'd just committed not to quit, whatever came of her thoughts.

She cleaned his house as usual and he made himself scarce the rest of the time. She left his bedroom for last and resolutely ignored the way her panties grew damp as she made his bed.

Want to read more? Beauty Touched the Beast is available at Amazon.com, BarnesAndNoble.com, and iBooks.

Other Books by Skye Warren

Wanderlust

On the Way Home

Prisoner

Dark Erotica Series

Keep Me Safe

Trust in Me

Hear Me

Don't Let Go

The Beauty Series

Beauty Touched the Beast

Beneath the Beauty

Broken Beauty

Beauty Becomes You

The Beauty Series Compilation

Standalone Erotic Romance

His for Christmas

Take the Heat: A Criminal Romance Anthology

Sweetest Mistress

Below the Belt

Dystopia Series

Leashed

Caged

About the Author

Skye Warren is the New York Times and USA Today Bestselling author of dark romance. Her books are raw, sexual and perversely romantic.

Sign up for Skye's newsletter:
www.skyewarren.com/newsletter

Like Skye Warren on Facebook:
facebook.com/skyewarren

Follow Skye Warren on Twitter:
twitter.com/skye_warren

Visit Skye's website for her current booklist:
www.skyewarren.com

ACKNOWLEDGEMENTS

Thank you to Shari Slade, Annika Martin, Sharon Muha, and Leanne Schafer for your knowledge—and bottomless patience!

COPYRIGHT

This is a work of fiction. Any resemblance to actual persons, living or dead, business establishments, events or locales is entirely coincidental. All rights reserved. Except for use in a review, the reproduction or use of this work in any part is forbidden without the express written permission of the author.

His for Christmas © 2014 by Skye Warren
Print Edition

Cover design by Book Beautiful
Formatting by BB eBooks

ISBN: 9781505814637

Made in the USA
Lexington, KY
05 May 2016